Volatile

Reactive Magic Book Three

Helen Vivienne Fletcher

First published in this format by HVF Publishing in 2022
Copyright © Helen Vivienne Fletcher, 2022
Edited by Jess Senior

ISBN:
978-1-99-116724-8 (paperback)
978-1-99-116725-5 (mobi)
978-1-99-116726-2 (epub)
978-1-99-116727-9 (large print)

This one is for Stella.

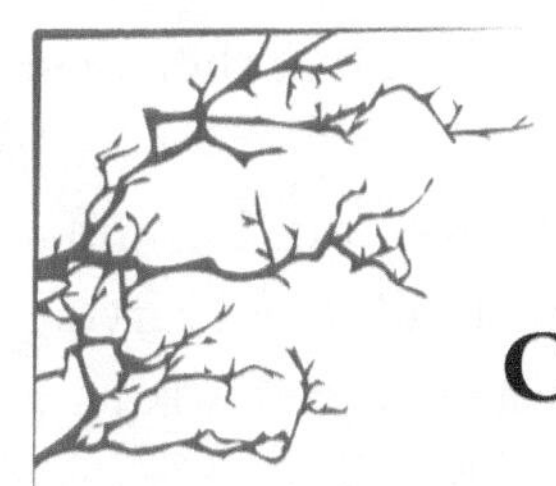

Chapter One

Ursula Trager – Age 14

The beating of hammers sent rumbles through the floor beneath my feet. Thumps vibrated in my chest, a rhythmic beat that shook me. It made it hard to think, unsettling me as energy tingled in little pulses.

I stood at the window, watching. The students wouldn't arrive for another few hours, but anticipation charged the air, mingling with the sounds of the building work below me. If I were more comfortable wielding magic, I would be able to use this, to turn it into something spectacular. I closed my eyes, imagining that the vibrations came from the earth itself. I inhaled, pretending I could feel the movement of the very planet.

"Grow," I whispered.

Immediately, dread built in my stomach. I opened my eyes a crack, terrified I would see darkness – vines covering the windows, or trees having sprouted up to block out the light. Instead, I was greeted with the exact same view I had seen all my life.

Soon, I told myself. Soon, things would change.

The thumping from downstairs had increased as my parents sought to get the school finished before the students got here. The chances of that happening were low, given they were arriving today, but still my parents persisted.

Footsteps clattered on the stairs down the corridor, and a moment later Chloe burst into my room, blonde braid carving an arc in the air around her shoulders like a weapon. "What are you doing?" she asked. She moved to stand beside me, her gaze flicking to the window.

I stepped back from it. "Nothing," I said, not willing to admit I had spent the whole morning staring out. A slow, sly smile spread across her face.

"They're not coming here for *you*," she said.

I felt my cheeks flush. "I know that." I did know that, but it didn't stop me hoping.

Chloe let out a little giggle. "Whatever you say." She turned, flouncing towards the door. "Mum and Dad want to see us downstairs. But do something with your hair first, you look a mess." She didn't wait for me, her feet clattering down the next set of stairs before I'd even crossed the room.

My fair hair was a mirror image of Chloe's, though somehow it never looked as nice, hanging limply around my shoulders. I pulled it into a ponytail – practical and less deadly than Chloe's braid – and smoothed out my crumpled T-shirt. Chloe didn't seem to care whether or not I followed, but I trailed after her anyway. The heat in my cheeks didn't cool as I circled down the flights of stairs. I hated that she was right. I *was* hoping that the students arriving would be at least a tiny bit interested in me. But they wouldn't be. No one ever was.

I came out into the entryway of our house. That still looked the same at least – high ceilings and skylights looking down over Mum's ever-increasing collection of houseplants. If she kept this up, soon it would be more greenhouse than foyer.

Muddy footprints crossed the black and white tiles, one of the builders leaving their mark. All around us, workers were transforming home into school. They might as well have been carving off pieces of my flesh. I dreaded seeing the cosy spaces of my childhood turned into sterile classrooms. At least our bedrooms were staying the same. Our floor would be left untouched, a safe place in all this chaos.

Dad stood in the middle of the foyer, Chloe and Ben facing each other in front of him. My stomach gave a flip, and I contemplated turning tail and running back up to my room.

"Ursula, get down here," Dad's voice rang out before I could. "Your sister might be about to beat Ben for once."

Chloe grimaced, and I reluctantly made my way down the last few steps. Ben gave me a wink, which was more than Chloe would ever do, but it was brief, his focus turning away almost immediately. My brother and sister both raised their palms, a glow forming between them.

"Over here, love." Mum reached out, drawing me to the side. I took her hand, gratefully. Magic crackled in the room, not helped by the continued pulsing of hammers.

"Unless you want to help Chloe?" Dad asked. "Perhaps the two of you would be a match for your brother."

I shrank behind Mum, and I felt her stiffen. Dad's voice held a laugh, but I didn't trust him not to actually force me into it. I hated when he made them fight, and my mother's cries of "Ursula's too young for this" wouldn't protect me for much longer.

Chloe's hands trembled, the colour emanating from them shuddering. She kept up a good fight, but she wouldn't beat him. She was too focused on trying to use force. My brother just made himself immovable, drawing magic from everything around him until Chloe tired herself out.

My father made a noise in his throat. "Come on, Chloe! Don't be so weak."

Sweat beaded on her forehead, and Dad's lip quirked, delighting in Ben's victory already. Mum's hand tightened on mine, but she didn't say anything. *She's not weak,* I wanted to yell. *Ben's just stronger.* But Chloe wouldn't appreciate me speaking up any more than Dad would.

"Steel yourself!" Dad yelled. "Don't let him force you back."

Chloe's legs shook, her physical strength waning along with her magic. Mum's plants drooped as Ben pulled energy from them, and Chloe stumbled backwards, her magical glow disappearing.

"Yes!" Dad's arms flew into the air. "Unbeaten!"

None of that delight lit Ben's face. He watched Chloe, concern creasing his forehead. "You okay, kiddo?"

"Shut up!" Chloe shoved him, no magic, just fury in her hands this time. "I'm not a kid."

Ben dodged backwards out of her way, a half laugh escaping him. "Okay, okay! Clearly, you're a mature adult."

"Don't be a sore loser, Chloe. You just have to accept your brother is better than you." Dad patted Ben on the back, congratulating him, and Ben's jaw tightened in response. I could see in Dad's eyes that he wanted to make them try again, despite the fact that Chloe was still shaking. For once, I was glad to be almost invisible. I couldn't do that a single time, let alone as often as my father wanted.

"We had some things to discuss," Mum said quietly. She picked up one of her plants, grimacing as she inspected its withered state.

"Hm? Oh yes, come, come." Dad moved to stand next to Mum, drawing us to him. I had an urge to line up next to my brother and sister in height order, like we were the von Trapp children. I couldn't see Chloe ever singing songs on the mountain though, and she definitely wouldn't wear dresses made from curtains.

"The new students will be arriving here this afternoon," Dad announced. He said that like we were students ourselves. We were his children, but perhaps he'd forgotten that in his excitement over the strength of Ben and Chloe's powers. "This will be a new era in our family's magic, and I want you all to make the most of it."

Chloe rolled her eyes and gave a snort. It annoyed me that she was acting like she was above all this. She was half the reason our parents had decided we needed magic training in the first place. If she and Ben had just kept things simple, Mum and Dad might not have made such a big deal out of everything.

Dad gave Chloe a hard look. "I'm expecting you to welcome the new students. You need to learn from them – become as strong as you can be."

"They've had just as hard a time of it as you have with developing powers," Mum added quietly. "Harder maybe, since they didn't have the benefit of parents who know about magic."

Ben made a noise in his throat which could have been agreement or irritation. "We'll do everything we can to make them feel comfortable."

Mum smiled at him, ignoring the hint of sarcasm in his voice. "I know you will, darling." She gave me a warm smile too and squeezed my shoulder. I relaxed a little at her touch. We were still a family. Becoming a school didn't have to change that.

"Excellent." Dad clapped his hands together as if dismissing us. He started to walk away, heading off to yell at some of the workers no doubt, but then called back over his shoulder. "You should be excited about the lessons, Chloe. You might actually learn to beat your brother."

Chloe scowled, and I felt my face form a similar expression. I hated the way he goaded her. Chloe turned to Mum as soon as he was gone. "Why couldn't you just get us private lessons?" she whined. "Why did you have to build a whole school?"

"It's not just about the three of you, love." Weariness filled Mum's voice. This wasn't the first time she'd had this argument with my sister. "Your magic is twinned with theirs; geminus magic has the potential to be very dangerous if not handled correctly."

Chloe rolled her eyes. "I just don't get why it's our responsibility."

Literally for the reason Mum just said, I thought, but I kept my mouth firmly shut.

"Of course you don't." My brother took up the eye rolling. "You don't think anything is your responsibility."

Chloe flushed a little, but she held Ben's gaze, refusing to back down. He didn't take the bait, turning to Mum. "Was that all you dragged us down here for?"

Mum blinked, perhaps deciding whether or not to chide Ben. He'd grown taller than her, surpassing Dad too, and he seemed to be forgetting all of us as he reached heights we couldn't.

"We thought you'd like to see the new classrooms," Mum said finally.

Chloe let out a long breath. "We're going to be stuck in them all week, aren't we? We don't need to start early."

Ben clearly agreed with the sentiment, but he and Mum stared at each other, a silent conversation passing between them. Then he looked at me, his face softening. "Do you want to see them, Ursula?"

I hesitated. Choosing to go with Ben would piss Chloe off, but honestly, everything I did pissed her off. I looked to Mum instead. She gave a little smile. "It might make you feel better to see the changes now, love."

Ben squeezed my shoulder. "Come on, I'll race you." He bolted up the stairs, giving himself a head start, not that he needed it. I chased after him, Mum's laughter and Chloe's snort of derision following after us.

THE NEW ROOMS WERE not that interesting. My parents had turned the floor below ours into a dormitory of sorts, where the new students would sleep, then the bottom two floors were now a series of classrooms. The house had always been far too big for us, and the changes made it feel not only vast but sterile.

We didn't stay long in the classrooms. The huge shelves of textbooks and rows of desks made me feel odd. There were only three students coming, but so many desks – a visible sign of my parents' unspoken plans.

"Make sure you stay out of Dad's way this week," Ben said, as we passed a couple of builders in the corridor.

"I *always* try to stay out of Dad's way," I told him.

Ben frowned. He opened his mouth, but then closed it again without speaking. "Good idea," he said finally. "Keep doing that."

I followed him upstairs into the dormitory. "If we're supposed to stay close to the new students to help their magic, why are they sleeping on a different floor?"

Ben snorted. "Can you imagine asking Chloe to share a room?"

I laughed at the thought. "She doesn't even like sharing a wall with me."

Ben grinned. "Eh, you're not so bad. Just like having a little mouse live next door." He reached out, ruffling my hair.

I squirmed away. My gaze fell on the door at the end of the hallway. Jagged black marks spread out across the walls around it, and streaks of ash surrounded the doorhandle. "What happened to the library?"

Ben didn't look up. "Don't worry about it. Mum and Dad moved the important books downstairs."

"But the door..." I took a few steps forward. I couldn't explain it, but there was something wrong with the air at the end of the corridor. I couldn't see anything exactly, but it *felt* different. There was a dull sort of... *nothing* to it, as if it wasn't real. It seemed to suck inwards, like a black hole or a vacuum. I took another step towards it.

"Don't!" Ben's hand slammed down on my shoulder.

I gasped, cringing away from him. His face fell, and he crouched down, pulling me into a hug. "I'm sorry, Urse. I didn't mean to scare you."

"Why...?" The question died on my lips.

Ben sighed. He shifted so he could look me in the eye. "You heard about the fire?"

I nodded. My siblings' experiments with magic had gone very wrong. I hadn't been there when it happened, but as far as I could gather, they'd tried to create indoor fireworks and nearly burnt the place to the ground. Not that their outdoor fireworks had been much better.

Ben nodded towards the library. "There was a lot of damage. Chloe and I fixed some of it with magic. That's probably what you can feel."

"Why can't I go down there if you fixed it?"

Ben gave a short laugh. "I said we fixed *some* of it. Neither of us are that good yet."

If the dull sucking feeling was anything to go by, they'd had no idea what they were doing. It didn't feel like they'd fixed anything, only charged it with a strange energy. I supposed Mum and Dad would be able to reverse it, and the builders could repair the physical damage once they were done with all the other work. "You didn't burn any of the books, did you?'

Ben grinned. "Only the evil ones." He gave my hair another ruffle and then sighed. "Do you want to see the rest of the dormitories?"

I could tell he had no interest in seeing them, and suddenly neither did I. "No. It feels weird to go into someone else's bedroom."

"True." Ben glanced at his watch. "Hey, I've got some stuff to finish before they arrive. Shall we head back up to our floor now?"

I nodded and followed Ben to the stairs. I paused in the doorway, looking back towards the library. That dull, empty feeling followed me down the corridor. I didn't like the idea of the new students sleeping with that right beside them. Then again, our magic was supposed to get stronger once we met our geminus pair – the person our magic was twinned to. Perhaps together, we'd be able to fix what Ben and Chloe had broken.

My stomach tensed. I'd been waiting days for my geminus pair to arrive, but what if they didn't like me? What if they were just like Chloe?

Ben glanced back at me. He followed my gaze down the hallway, and his face tightened. "Come on, little mouse," he said, forcing a smile. "Ready for another race? See if you can beat me this time." He took off, leaving me to chase after him. I pounded up the stairs, watching him get further and further away from me, with about a mouse's chance of catching up.

Chapter Two

Mum called us downstairs again that afternoon. My stomach flipped, knowing that this time it would be because the students were here. I trailed down the steps, passing workers carrying a large whiteboard up to the second-floor classrooms.

"Hi... yes, thanks," I said, as they stood back to let me pass.

Silence greeted my words, and I scurried past, getting out of their way. Their eyes all held a vague, glazed look, and they moved with a heavy lethargy as if the boredom of the work drained them of energy with every passing minute.

I made my way down the rest of the stairs and found Mum in the foyer. She ushered me out to join my siblings on the doorstep.

"Where's Dad?" I asked.

"He's talking to the builders. Don't worry about him." Her face switched back and forth between over-excited beam and nervous lip chewing.

Chloe rolled her eyes when she saw me. "You still look a mess, squirt."

I blushed, trying once again to smooth my clothes. Ben clucked his tongue. "Leave her alone, Chloe."

She made a face at him, then her expression returned to a practised, disinterested glare. Ben popped his lips, boredom etched across his whole body. They still both snuck eager looks every time an engine roared from the street, though.

Finally, a car pulled into the drive, and we all stood up straighter.

"Remember – be welcoming." Mum beamed at us. Ben and Chloe both rolled their eyes this time.

The car stopped at the base of the steps, but the doors didn't open. Through the tinted windows, I could just make out three figures – one in the front, two in the back. Chloe craned her neck to peer in, her attempt at nonchalance forgotten. The driver hugged the other two, and the back doors finally opened, a boy and a girl getting out.

"I didn't know they knew each other," Ben murmured.

"Hello! We're so glad you arrived safely." Mum moved forward to help them with their bags, but my siblings and I stayed frozen on the steps.

The girl turned towards us, dark wavy hair swishing across her shoulders in a way that was both messy and beautiful. She smiled at me, and I liked her instantly.

Chloe gasped. "Is she pregnant?"

Ben smacked Chloe's arm. "Be nice," he said, looking at both of us. I hadn't said anything; why was I getting told off?

The girl's face flushed, and the boy reached for her hand, pulling her close. I could see what Chloe meant. The girl's peasant dress rose abruptly at her waist as if covering a huge baby bump.

"Welcome." Mum took the girl's hand, drawing her towards the house. "These are my children, who will be joining you in the new school."

The girl glanced towards the boy as if seeking reassurance. He didn't notice, his dark eyes focused up at the house instead. He reminded me of Ben – tanned, athletic and projecting confidence... but in his own world, like he was above the rest of us.

Chloe stepped forward, surprising me. "Nice to meet you. I'm Chloe," she said. After a moment she seemed to remember us. "And this is my brother and sister, Ursula and Benjamin."

The girl looked to the boy again and this time he grinned. He dropped her hand to reach for Chloe's. "I'm Joe. This is Sammy."

Chloe looked Sammy up and down, her expression not altogether friendly. "So, are you pregnant?"

"Chloe!" Mum and Ben said at the same time.

Sammy seemed to shrink under our gaze. I wanted to say something – to reassure her – but I felt myself shrinking just as much as she was.

"Yes, we'll be having a baby in about a month," Joe said. He put his arm around Sammy, and she relaxed a little.

"How old are you?" I asked.

"Ursula!" Mum frowned at me. "That's not nice either."

"I didn't mean it like that. I just want to know..." I trailed off as Mum glared at me. All I wanted to find out was whether they were young enough to be my friends, or whether they would instantly dismiss me as "just a kid" like Ben and Chloe.

"Don't mind my sisters." Ben shook his head. "They don't get out much."

"It's okay," Sammy said. "We're both seventeen. We know we're young to be parents." She fiddled with a collection of silver bangles around her wrist, then looked to Joe as if she wanted him to add something, but he was back to staring up at the house.

Seventeen – older than Chloe, and just younger than my brother's eighteen years. Sammy seemed nice, but if it came down to it, she'd be far more eager to hang out with my brother and sister than with me.

"How old are you?" Sammy asked me.

"Fourteen," I mumbled. Chloe often reminded me I looked more like twelve.

"Come on in. We'll show you to your rooms." Chloe aimed this towards Joe, ignoring the rest of us.

"There's one more student to arrive," Mum said.

Chloe gave another eye roll and shifted her weight into a posture that screamed irritation. Honestly, I was starting to feel the same way.

"So you both have magic, huh?" Ben asked.

Mum shot Ben a frown as he asked this, but she didn't interrupt. Joe and Sammy looked at each other, a whole conversation seeming to happen behind their eyes.

"A little," Joe said, finally.

Obviously, that wasn't true. I didn't need to be an expert in body language to notice the lies, but even without that, they must have had more than a little magic to get noticed by my parents.

Ben raised his eyebrows. "Oh yeah? What can you do?"

Joe and Sammy glanced at each other again. At first, I thought they were going to refuse, but then Joe closed his eyes. Little daisies peeked up through the grass around us. He didn't stop there. Tiny plants crept out through the gaps in the concrete path as well, stretching up to greet us.

He let out a breath, opening his eyes. "I'm good with plants," he said. He lent down, picking one of the flowers and handing it to Sammy. She smiled, getting even prettier as she blushed.

Chloe wrinkled her nose, but I could tell she was impressed. Ben regarded Joe, his assessment of him clearly rising at least a few points too. He turned to Sammy. "What about you?" he asked.

Sammy opened her mouth, but Joe squeezed her hand, stopping her. "Can't give away all our secrets now, can we?" He raised his eyebrows and grinned.

If anything, this seemed to impress my brother even more. Chloe just stared at Sammy, her eyes narrowing slightly.

Another car turned in to the driveway – an older, beaten-up wreck that made a chugging noise like it was barely running. It pulled up in the same spot as the first car, barely stopping before a back door flew open, no pauses for goodbye hugs. A boy leapt out, dragging an oversized duffel bag with him.

I stepped back, the chaos of his energy confusing me. His dark curly hair bounced around him for a moment after he came to a stop, and his long, black eyelashes flickered as he stared up at the house. "Jeepers." His jaw dropped open. "They didn't tell me I was coming to a mansion!"

A laugh burst out of me, and Ben pressed his lips together, trying not to follow suit. I could see the others were holding back sniggers at the word "jeepers" too. The kid's eyes finally travelled down from the house to meet ours. The laughter died in my throat as his gaze met mine. His eyes were beautiful, but full of that same chaotic energy, making my heart pound.

He blinked and his face brightened. He bounced forward to greet us – like actually bounced, there was no other way to describe it.

"I'm Arthur. Pleased to meet you. Arthur Grandace." He held out his hand to my mum.

"Welcome," she said. "I'm Candace Trager. I spoke with your parents."

My brother grinned, clearly taking a liking to the kid. He held out his hand. "Benjamin."

"Arthur," Arthur said again. He moved down the line, shaking hands, which elicited further giggles from the others as they mumbled their names. I found myself shrinking back, dreading him reaching for my hand.

Thankfully, Ben picked up Arthur's bag before he got to me. "Come on." Ben nodded towards the house. "I'll introduce you to the rest of this lot properly inside."

"Wait, wait," Mum called. "I want to get a picture of you all. We have to commemorate your first day at magic school!"

The others all either groaned or laughed, but let Mum gather them together for a photo on the steps. "Everyone say cheese!"

I forced my lips to stretch into something resembling a smile, but inside my stomach tightened. *Our first day of magic school.* This was supposed to be a happy thing, and it mostly was. I just couldn't help thinking it might also be my last day of family.

MUM ASKED US TO GIVE the new students a tour. Arthur kept up a steady chatter as we walked up the stairs. Ben joked and laughed with him, while Chloe rolled her eyes behind his back.

Sammy and Joe kept to themselves. She seemed to be having some trouble with the stairs, and he hung back to walk with her, the two of them speaking quietly in a way that didn't involve the rest of us. I walked between the two groups, already unsure of where I fit.

"This is where you'll sleep," Ben told them. "You can pick your own rooms."

"Cool." Arthur took off through one of the doorways. A moment later, there was a thump as he jumped on the bed.

Sammy and Joe looked at each other, then at the remaining two doorways. I felt awkward, as I realised they were deciding whether or not to share a room. Seventeen was only three years older than me, but Joe and Sammy's world felt an entire lifetime away from mine.

"What's down there?" Sammy asked. She stared down the corridor towards the blackened door.

I'd almost forgotten about the library, but as soon as Sammy mentioned it, that strange, empty feeling tugged at me again.

"Nothing," Chloe said quickly.

Joe and Sammy both looked up at that, and Arthur's head poked around the doorway of his room. Way to make it seem more interesting, Chloe.

"Ignore her," Ben said. "We just screwed up some magic and she's embarrassed."

"Been there." Joe grinned, but Sammy's eyes drifted back to the door, tension clouding her face. I wondered if she could feel the same thing I could. The others didn't seem bothered by it.

"What are these marks on the floor?" Arthur asked. "Are they runes? I've been learning all about ancient languages. What do they say?"

Ben waited for the stream of questions to stop. "Yes, it's a rune line. My parents lay them around the house. Don't cross that one. In fact, don't go down that end of the corridor. The magic's still a bit volatile."

Chloe gave a snort. "It's not that bad!"

Ben raised an eyebrow. "She never thinks her failures are 'that bad'," he told the others.

The rune line hadn't been there this morning. The group began swapping magic-fail stories, laughing as they tried to top each other. I didn't have any of those, scared to try any of the showier spells Ben and Chloe seemed to favour. I slipped away from them, inching towards the rune line. I stopped when I reached it, but stretched out my foot, touching a toe to the symbols etched on the floor. Buzzing zapped through me.

"That's powerful," a quiet voice said beside me.

I started, turning to see Sammy. I hadn't realised she'd followed me. She glanced back at the group. Joe hadn't come with her. He stood with Ben, coaxing a vine he'd created to grow up the wall.

"It's just a rune line," I told Sammy.

She shook her head. "I mean what's behind that door. I don't like the idea of sleeping next to it."

I nodded. It's what I'd thought this morning. "I'm sure Mum and Dad will fix it soon."

"Yeah." Sammy's voice didn't hold that much conviction. She looked like she wanted to say something else, but she drifted back towards the group instead. She folded her arms over her bump, holding herself tightly as if trying to ward off the magic.

I waited until she was absorbed, talking to Joe, then I crouched down, examining the symbols on the floor. They were well formed, but not as strong as I would have liked. I closed my eyes and ran my hand over the line.

Relax, I said to myself, releasing the mental stranglehold I used to keep my power hidden and contained. My magic began to flow, and I poured protection into each symbol, doubling what my parents had started.

I opened my eyes. The vacuum feeling from the library eased – still there, but now only as background noise. I smiled, the anxious rush in my head quietening now the magic was contained. I turned to go back to the group.

They were still deep in conversation, swapping stories and showing off little spells. All except Chloe.

My sister's eyes flicked between me and the rune line, a scowl on her face. She didn't speak, letting the silence hang heavy between us, but I could tell she'd seen what I'd done. She knew exactly how powerful my magic really was.

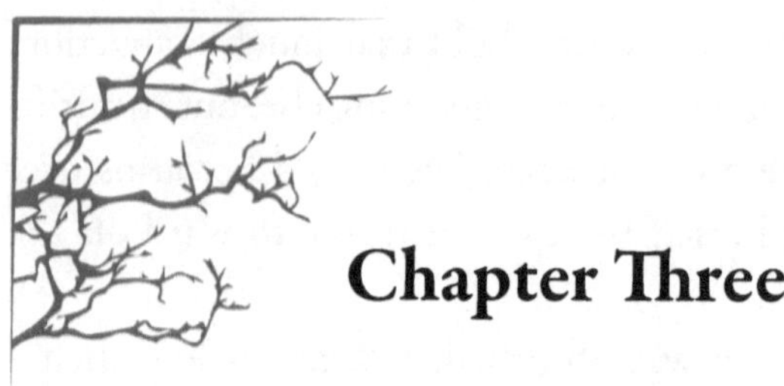

Chapter Three

I woke early the next day, but skipped breakfast, too nervous to eat. Today, we would be entering the classroom as students for the first time. I brushed my hair in front of the window, watching my reflection in the glass. A single ivy vine had crept up over the window frame overnight, clinging to the flaking paint. For a moment, I feared my magic had coaxed it to grow, my ill-conceived, impulsive spell from the previous morning finally taking effect, but it was more likely down to Joe or Sammy.

I wound my hair into two tight braids, even though it played into Chloe's comments about me looking young. Today I wanted my sister to see me as little – vulnerable.

My throat went dry as I thought of the moment with the rune line. Would Chloe tell Dad what she'd seen? I couldn't bear to think what he'd do if he knew I'd been hiding how powerful my magic really was.

I ran my hands down my T-shirt and shorts, smoothing them out, then made my way out into the corridor and down the first set of stairs, trying to calm myself with the thudding rhythm of my steps. Perhaps it would have worked, but a shout from downstairs had my heart pounding again – Dad, yelling at some of the workers. Power boomed in his voice, and his fierce magic expanded through the building.

I froze, considering turning tail, but it was too late. A group of builders trudged up the stairs towards me, Dad leading the way. He caught sight of me but gave me only a cursory glance. The workers didn't acknowledge me at all, filing past with uniform, dragging steps. They looked like zombies, shambling after Dad.

I stumbled on the next stair, something sticking in my throat. *Were* they zombies? Was my dad controlling them with his magic, forcing them to work to exhaustion in the pursuit of finishing his perfect school?

I stared up at the trail of people, disappearing onto the floor above me. No... surely, he wouldn't do that. I swallowed, hard, but the tight feeling in my throat didn't clear. My father was a man who made his own children fight. Could I really put anything past him?

The dormitory-floor door burst open next to me, sending me skittering back a pace. I blinked, all thoughts of zombies shambling away on their own.

"Ursula." Sammy's voice was high and tight, and her cheeks held a bright flush. "Why are you standing in the stairwell?" She shook her head, not waiting for an answer. "You haven't seen a notebook, have you?"

"I don't think so."

Sammy let out a puff of air. "I'm sure I brought it. I *know* I brought it. It must have fallen out of my bags."

"Maybe Mum has it? If she does, she'll bring it to the classroom." Hopefully it would just be Mum visiting us today. I'd rather Dad stayed as far away as possible.

Sammy nodded, but she chewed on her lip. She fell into pace beside me, circling down the next flight of stairs to the classrooms. Her silver bangles clattered together, creating a tinkling soundtrack to her steps.

"Is it your diary?" I asked. "The notebook, I mean."

Sammy shook her head. "Not exactly."

I waited, but she didn't offer any further explanation. We made our way down the stairs in silence, our feet hitting the floor in unison and her jangling jewellery the only interruption to it.

I took a breath before stepping into the classroom, steeling myself. The room had changed even since yesterday, becoming more sterile. A large whiteboard had been installed, dominating the front wall of the room, and an imposing teacher's desk planted in front of it. I pictured a terrifying figure standing behind it, school master from my nightmares.

"Morning!" Arthur called. He stood staring up at the wall of textbooks, eagerness lighting his face.

"Morning," I mumbled back, but he didn't seem to hear. His eyes traced over the spines, widening occasionally as a title caught his attention. Chloe sat on one of the desks, an exercise book in her hand.

Sammy stopped dead in the doorway, her face turning pale. I glanced between her and Chloe. "Is that...?"

Chloe looked up, her eyes landing on me. "Is this yours, little mouse?" she asked, raising the notebook. "What's so secret you're writing in code?"

"Give that back!" I grabbed for the book, but Chloe held it out of my reach.

"Calm down, it's not like I was reading it. What even is this?"

"It's not yours, that's what it is." I reached for the book again, and Chloe dodged out of my way.

"Touchy-touchy!" She flipped through the pages, pretending to read them. The spine bent back, threatening to rip.

"I said, give it back!"

Chloe held the book above her head, and danced backwards, waving it side to side like a little kid. "How ever are you going to get your book back?" she said with mock concern. "If only your magic was stronger."

I froze. Chloe smirked, and I cursed myself for giving her the reaction she wanted. She wouldn't tell Dad about my magic, would she? Not over something like this?

"It's not Ursula's book; it's mine," Sammy said quietly.

Chloe's eyes widened. "I..." For a moment, it seemed like she would apologise, then something else crossed her face. She smiled – a twisted, mean smirk. "Well, that still doesn't explain why *you're* writing things in code, Samantha."

Joe and Ben chose that moment to walk into the room. Joe grinned as he saw Sammy, then his expression fell, taking in the tension in the room. "Hey, is something wrong?"

I ignored him, still focused on my sister. She made a show of flicking through the notebook pages. "Maybe my parents should know about..." Chloe trailed off, something in the pages catching her eye. "Their magic will flare out of control," she said softly to herself, reading. "And she will realise..." she cut herself off abruptly, her eyes widening.

"What's going on?" Ben asked.

"Chloe stole Sammy's notebook," Arthur said, before anyone else could speak. I looked up. He still stood by the bookshelf, silent the entire time we'd been arguing. So strange that he had so much energy, such eagerness and frenetic movement, yet managed to disappear into stillness when it suited him.

Chloe blinked, dragging her eyes away from the page. "Don't be so dramatic. I didn't steal it; I found it."

Ben grabbed the book from her hand. "Cut it out, Chloe. You're not seven." He glanced down, and his gaze caught in the same way Chloe's had. His eyes flicked across the page, reading, then his expression hardened into something I couldn't interpret. He looked up at Sammy. She'd gone pale again, fear sparking in her eyes. She reached out for the book. Ben hesitated, then handed it over.

Joe touched Sammy's shoulder. "Are you okay?"

Sammy nodded, clutching the book to her chest. His arm slid around her shoulder, pulling her into a hug. Something shifted in the room, everything becoming charged. A look passed between Chloe and Ben, then her eyes flicked towards Sammy. Whatever they'd read, it seemed to have unsettled both of them.

But the book was back in Sammy's hands, where it should be. I sank down into one of the desks, all of the fight going out of me. Funny how things worked like that. I could barely hold a conversation, shyness sticking the words in my throat, but when someone was threatened, I could argue for them, *fight* for them.

Arthur slid into the chair next to me. "Are you okay?" he asked. I frowned, anticipating some kind of punchline, but he stared back at me, his dark eyes open and curious.

"Yeah, I'm fine," I said. "My sister can just be..." I let that hang, the end of the sentiment clear enough without me having to say it.

I stared down at the desktop. My parents had bought the desks from a local high school, and they were covered in scribbles, layers of pen scraped into the surface. Was this something we were supposed to do too? Carve our mark into the furniture to prove we'd been here?

Suddenly, it felt important to do just that. I took out a pen, pressing hard and carving my initials on top of all the others. Arthur watched me, probably puzzling at my strange actions. I dropped the pen as soon as I was done. It landed with a clatter, bouncing off the table. Arthur picked it up. He leaned over, adding his own initials below mine.

"You're nervous," he said. It wasn't a question.

I swallowed. "Is this what schools are normally like?"

His eyebrows rose a little in surprise, and I blushed. I shouldn't have said that – shouldn't have admitted I had no understanding of such a normal thing. Mum and Dad always said we'd learn more in home school. Now I knew about the geminus magic, I wondered if the choice to keep us out of regular school had been made simply to avoid us accidentally killing other kids.

"Mostly," Arthur said finally. "It's never going to be completely normal with magic, though, right?"

We would never be completely normal with magic.

"All right, children." A firm voice rang out from the hallway, and a young woman stepped through the doorway, high heels clicking against the floor. "Come take a seat. My name is Miss Caraway, and I will be your instructor in magic."

Joe and Sammy extracted themselves from each other's arms, and everyone settled into seats. I snuck looks at Miss Caraway. She wore a thin, floral dress – not the sort of thing

I would have expected with that loud voice – and soft, curly hair bounced around her shoulders. She looked sweet, but that wasn't exactly a good thing when it came to teaching my sister. I had a feeling Chloe would have her in tears by the end of the first week.

"In the coming months, other instructors will arrive to teach you in the traditional subjects, but for now we are focused on gaining control of your powers."

I turned to Arthur. "Do you think she's a—"

"No talking, please." Miss Caraway's voice snapped with a force that had to have magic behind it. I shrank automatically, and Chloe let out a giggle, earning herself a stern look.

I took a breath, letting it out slowly. This would be okay – it had to be. Whatever Miss Caraway's style of teaching, it couldn't be worse than Dad's.

Miss Caraway looked at each of us, in turn, her gaze serious. "As you know, the six of you hold magic."

"Hell yeah, we do," Joe said. He raised his chair, levitating it an inch off the floor. His magic wasn't strong enough to hold him, and he came clattering back down.

Miss Caraway raised her eyebrows. "Yes, quite."

I suppressed a smile. I'd underestimated her. It would take at least *two* weeks for Chloe to have her in tears.

"Joseph, is it?" Miss Caraway asked.

Joe nodded, feet firmly on the ground now. "Joe."

"All right, Joe. You will probably have already noticed that your magic is somewhat unreliable?"

Chloe looked at me when Miss Caraway said that, but I didn't return her gaze.

"Yeah, I guess," Joe mumbled.

"This is an unfortunate side effect of geminus magic," Miss Caraway continued. "You've heard this term, yes?"

Only about a hundred times. The way Dad went on, it was like he thought we'd won the magic lottery. Mum seemed more concerned one of us was going to blow up.

"Our magic is twinned with another person's," Sammy said.

"Indeed," Miss Caraway said. "Your magic will be stronger and more stable when paired with another person's. Alone, you will struggle to control it – for some geminus magic wielders, their magic will fade completely if they don't find their pair, but that is best case scenario. In other cases, it becomes danger-ous. Explosive even."

Perhaps that explained why my siblings had been so drawn to making fireworks.

"So how do we stop that?" Arthur asked.

Miss Caraway smiled, evidently appreciating the sensible question. "Before we do anything else, I think it would be a good idea if you all get to know your pair a little better."

My heart did a leap then started to hammer. I snuck a look at Arthur, but he didn't look back at me.

"Joseph, you'll be with Chloe," Miss Caraway said.

Chloe blinked, and Joe raised his head, surprise taking over his usual self-assured expression. "I thought I'd be with Sam-my."

Miss Caraway shook her head. "No. The magic is strongly indicating you are twinned with Chloe."

Sammy looked towards Chloe and frowned. Her eyes flicked back to Joe. "Then who am I paired with?"

"Your magic seems to be gravitating towards Ursula's."

Sammy looked around at me as if she had forgotten I was even there. She caught herself and schooled her face into a smile. "I'm sure we'll work really well together."

"Have fun babysitting." Chloe smirked at Sammy then turned her gaze on me. I glared back at her for a moment before I wavered and dropped my gaze.

"I guess that leaves me and Arthur." Ben got up, moving over to sit next to Arthur.

"Neato," Arthur said. My brother suddenly became very focused on wiping something from his eye. I couldn't tell how he felt about it, other than being amused by Arthur's excited exclamation. Then again, I'm not sure any of us knew how we felt about these matches yet.

"Hey." Sammy made her way over to my desk. "I'm glad we're working together. Hopefully it will mean great things for both of our magic."

Shyness overcame me, and I found I couldn't do anything except smile. Even that may have come out as more of a mouth shrug. I felt Ben's eyes on me, then he leaned over across the aisle from his desk to say something to Sammy. I didn't hear what it was, but she smiled at him and then nodded. My cheeks flushed, knowing he was probably warning her I was socially inept.

She turned back to me. "Thanks for helping me before – with my book."

I nodded, though I hadn't actually got it back for her. She tilted her head to the side, clearly waiting for me to say something.

"You're welcome," I choked out eventually.

She smiled. "Ursula's a pretty name."

"No, it's not," I said automatically.

Sammy looked horrified, and I started to laugh. She joined me, a grin spreading across her face.

"If we're twinned, does that mean I'm connected to your baby's magic as well?" I blurted out. I glanced at her stomach, and then pressed my lips together, shushing myself. Maybe I still wasn't supposed to mention it.

Sammy just looked thoughtful. "I don't know. I don't even know if she'll have magic yet."

I nodded, running out of questions. Her focus had turned to the notebook she'd taken back from Chloe. She thumbed through it, reading, then drew a star in the margin. I glanced down at the page, but I couldn't make out her handwriting.

I snuck a look at what the others were doing. Chloe and Joe had their palms pressed together in front of them, in the same way as when Dad made her and Ben fight. Chloe's had her eyelids lightly closed, but Joe kept blinking, as if unsure of what he was supposed to be doing. I felt the magic building between their hands from where I sat.

I looked back at Sammy. Should magic be growing between us too? But of course, it wouldn't unless I released mine. I took a breath, easing my grip on my power. Suddenly, I felt a tug at my stomach. A glowing rope of energy lit up between me and Sammy, like an umbilical cord joining us. I glanced around at the others, spotting similar cords growing between Chloe and Joe, and Ben and Arthur.

"The geminus connections," I whispered.

"Huh?" Sammy drew her eyes away from my brother. He and Arthur tossed a balled-up piece of paper back and forth between them. They'd levitated it and used their power to fling it from side to side, both of them laughing.

"We should set it on fire!" Arthur said, way too loudly. I shuddered at the thought.

"Can you do that sort of thing?" Sammy asked me.

I shrugged. "Maybe. I've never tried." I'd kept my magic use to a minimum around Dad. Besides, "fireball" didn't sound like much fun to me.

"I can't," Sammy told me. "My magic doesn't work like that."

Strangely, I could tell she had a lot of power, though it was a different sort to my brother and sister's. They seemed to gather energy to them, pulling it from everything around them when they wanted to do something. Sammy's just hummed quietly on her skin, coming from inside. I liked it. It was calming to be around.

Miss Caraway gasped. "What are you doing? Stop!"

I spun around. Chloe's hands glowed, colour flaring around them too bright to look at, but Joe's had turned black. Dark, ashy colour crept up his arms, his limbs withering under its touch. Chloe's eyes glazed over, reflecting the light.

"Joe!" Sammy shot out of her chair, but I stepped in front of her, shielding her as sparks shot out from Chloe's hands. "Oh god," Sammy whispered. "She's draining his energy!"

"I said stop!" Miss Caraway grabbed Chloe's shoulders, yanking her away. The light around Chloe flared, and Miss Caraway jerked, a shudder running through her. She fell backwards almost in slow motion. A choked sound rasped through her lips.

"Miss Caraway!" I ran towards her but stopped just short of touching her. Dark veins crept up from her fingertips, her skin blackening.

"No, don't touch him!" Ben yelled.

I spun around, just as Arthur grabbed Joe's shrivelled wrist. Colour flared out from Chloe's hands, engulfing Arthur's. I shielded my eyes, the glow too bright. A rune lit up on the inside of my eyelids.

Arthur shuddered. He turned towards me, and it seemed to take forever. Behind him, another surge of bright colour flared in Chloe's hands.

"Arthur!" I darted forward.

Sammy scrambled after me. "Ursula, don't!"

I caught hold of Arthur as the flare of colour faded, and yanked him back before another could surge. He swayed under my pull, dead weight resisting my rescue. Sammy caught his head before it smashed into the floor.

"Did it get you?" Ben grabbed my wrists, examining my hands. "Are you okay?"

I stared down at my palms. My skin remained pale, no signs of the dark ash. "I'm fine," I said. "I'm okay." I looked back at the others – at their blackened, withered flesh. Why hadn't it affected me? I felt magic tingling in my fingers, scratching against my skin.

Chloe blinked as if waking, and the light died down to a weak glow around her hands. She took in the slumped forms of our classmates and teacher, her eyes going wide. "What happened?"

"What do you think, Chloe?" Ben spat the words at her.

Blood trickled from Miss Caraway's nose, but her eyes were open, blinking. Arthur's fingers stretched out, as if still trying to catch the paper ball, his skin black and crumbly, desiccating in front of us.

I grabbed his hand on impulse. It felt warm to the touch, but something cold rushed through his veins. A tunnel of icy air opened up inside him, and I felt myself falling into it.

"No," I whispered. I pulled back, scrambling to escape, but Arthur kept falling.

Sammy grasped my other hand. She closed her eyes, pouring all of her magic into me, and I squeezed my eyes shut too. Something warm built inside me – warm, then hot, and then boiling. It rushed in my veins, pushing against the chill in Arthur's blood.

"My hands!" Joe gasped.

I opened my eyes. Colour rushed back into Joe's skin – into Arthur's and Miss Caraway's too. Arthur blinked at me, his healed hand tightening around mine.

Ben's mouth dropped open. "How are you doing that?"

I shook my head. "I... I don't know." I didn't loosen my grip on Arthur. In my mind, I saw his fingers crumbling, turning to ash between mine.

Ben stared at me for a moment longer, frowning, then he rounded on Chloe. "What were you thinking? You could have killed them."

Chloe shook her head, her face pale. "I don't know. I didn't mean to do anything."

"We just wanted to see if we could connect our magic." Joe balled his hands against his chest, as if protecting them. Sweat beaded on his forehead, and I was sure he was about to vomit. Suddenly, Miss Caraway groaned. She sat bolt upright, her whole body shivering.

"You're okay." Sammy knelt beside her, gently rubbing her arm. "It's all going to be okay." But Miss Caraway made a keening noise, that didn't sound okay at all.

Ben shook his head. "Mum and Dad are coming," he told Chloe. I could feel them moving towards us, drawn by the unusual magic.

Chloe went a shade paler, a shiver of her own working its way through her body. "I'm sorry," she whispered, and for once, I think she actually meant it.

Chapter Four

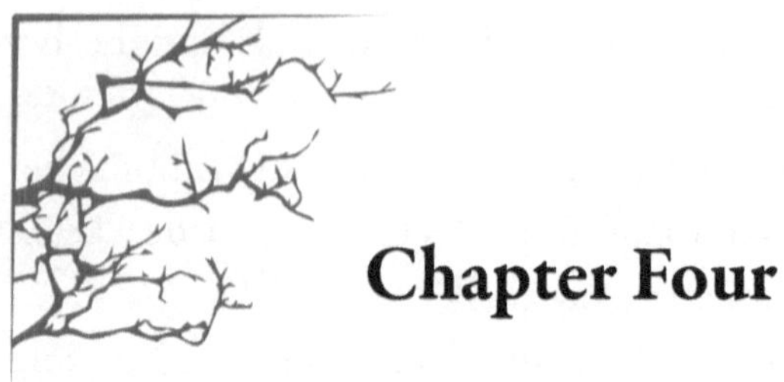

I stayed in bed late the next morning. My palms still itched with magic – the same magic that had protected me and saved my classmates. I stretched my fingers out, searching for its source. Nothing. I had no idea how I'd done it.

Then again, I hadn't done it alone.

Their magic will flare out of control... Chloe's words, read from Sammy's notebook, echoed in my mind. Sammy had been so sure of herself, grabbing my hand and joining her magic to mine. Had she known this was going to happen? If so, why hadn't she tried to stop it?

My parents had cancelled classes for the rest of the week, so Arthur, Joe and Miss Caraway could recover. Joe and Arthur didn't need it. Within hours of waking, Arthur had had a stream of questions about what happened, his magical curiosity far outweighing any ill effects he'd felt. As for Miss Caraway, I wasn't sure. My parents had whisked her away, and I wondered if my prediction about Chloe driving her to tears might have been a little too on the nose.

I got dressed, then stepped out into the corridor. Immediately, all the resolve flew out of me. I could go downstairs and demand to see Sammy's notebook, or I could march into my sister's room, and ask what exactly she thought she was doing draining Joe's energy like that. Instead, I stood, wavering as I tried to decide which option felt less impossible.

"What are you doing, brat?" Chloe's voice rang out from behind her bedroom door. It sat ajar, but knowing Chloe, that didn't constitute an invitation.

I pushed it open, not quite crossing the threshold. It had been a while since she'd let me in her room. Photos lined her walls, and I was surprised to see my own face peering out from some of them. In between the pictures, she'd hung band posters and images from magazines, creating an onslaught of colour.

She cleared her throat, and I snapped my gaze back to her. "Are you okay?" I asked her.

Chloe blinked, surprise chasing away her irritation. Had anyone else asked her that? We'd all been so concerned about the others, she'd been forgotten – or rather blamed – but yesterday had to have affected her too.

She shook her head, her expression returning to her regular disinterested glare. "I'm fine. You all overreacted. I would have got things under control if you'd given me another minute."

I frowned. "Really? It seemed like..." I trailed off as Chloe made another irritated noise in her throat.

Dark circles lined her eyes, and her cheeks were drawn. I doubted she'd got much sleep last night – I certainly hadn't. "What did you and Ben read in Sammy's notebook?" I asked.

She frowned. "Sammy's notebook..." she repeated. Her eyelids flickered, as if she was trying to dredge the memory from the depths of her mind, then she shook her head and shrugged. "I don't know. I don't remember. It was just some stream of consciousness nonsense, I think."

That didn't make sense. She and Ben had looked so worried by what they'd read, then part of it had come true. How could Chloe have just forgotten?

Suddenly, I noticed the way she was sitting, her hands cupped protectively over something, shielding it from my view. "What are you doing?"

Chloe wrinkled her nose like she was going to tell me to piss off, then her face softened. She beckoned me over. "Come here, I'll show you." She moved her hands, revealing a pair of white mice on the bedspread beside her.

I gasped. "Where did you get those? Mum will kill you if she sees rodents in the house."

Chloe rolled her eyes. "Well, you're not going to tell her, are you?"

I hesitated. I *probably* wasn't going to tell Mum. "Depends. What are you doing with them?"

Chloe grinned and shifted over in the bed so I could sit down. She held up her hand, a sparkling swirl of magic forming in her palm. It stretched out into a thin cord which wrapped itself around the mice. I tensed, my fingers digging into the bedspread.

A rune sparked in the air, disappearing again just as quickly. Chloe pulled on the end of the cord, leading the mice on a path across the bed. One of them followed willingly, seeming happy enough to go with the magical pull. The other's head twitched as if it was straining against her.

"How did you learn to do that?"

Chloe hesitated. "Joe showed me how to do it," she said finally. "My magic is getting stronger – must be the geminus connection. I think I might be able to lead a person eventually."

I recoiled, disgusted by the idea. Chloe didn't notice, her focus fixed on the mice and her Pied-Piper-like magic. She drew one of the mice closer to the side of the bed. In a second, it would topple over, walking straight over the edge into nothing.

"Stop it. You're hurting him!"

Chloe glanced up at me, her eyes widening. "No I'm not." The defensive note in her voice told me she had no idea whether this magic hurt the mice or not. She released them, and I gathered them up in my hands, stroking them gently. They cowered into me. "Where did you get them?"

Chloe's eyes flicked away from mine, and she shrugged. "Joe bought them at a pet shop in town."

"They're so little. You have to be careful." That wasn't what I wanted to say. I wanted her to stop completely – to let them go free.

She looked down at the little creatures in my hands. She reached out a finger, stroking their heads ever so gently. There was something in her expression I couldn't quite read – a heaviness that almost seemed like sadness. One of the mice sniffed her fingertip, and the hint of a smile crossed her lips.

"Maybe you're right," she said finally. She got up and pulled a small cage from her bedside drawer, holding it out to me. "Here."

I hesitated. I didn't want to surrender the animals to her, but what would I do with them otherwise? I studied her face. Her gaze was soft, repentant, and her shoulders slumped. "I promise I won't hurt them, okay? I was just trying to figure out the spell."

"Okay." I stretched out my hand and let the mice climb off it into their home. They scurried into their bed, happier once they were inside, though of course they didn't know who was holding the box. Chloe closed the lid and set it down on the top of her dresser. She placed her hand gently on the side of the cage as if offering an apology.

"So are Arthur and Joe okay?" she asked without turning around.

"I don't know. I was going to go down to the dorm and see how they're all doing."

"That's a good idea."

"Do you want to come with me?" I stepped out into the corridor.

Chloe took half a pace towards me, then stopped herself. Something shifted in her posture, and her lips quirked into a smirk. "Pass," she said.

I frowned. "Really? You don't want to—"

Chloe rolled her eyes. "I said *pass*. Leave me alone, brat." She closed the door, shutting me out. The sound of the latch clicking into place told me she wouldn't be opening it again anytime soon.

"What the...?" I stood for a moment, blinking at the closed door. What *was* that? The change in Chloe had been so sudden, like she'd flicked a switch and just didn't care anymore. I opened my mouth to yell at her, then shut it again without speaking. If she wasn't worried enough to check on our classmates after she hurt them, I couldn't make her. Besides, her trick with the mice made me nervous.

I turned away. Light flared from behind her door as I did. I glanced back, but the glow had faded, leaving behind only the tiniest streak of ash around the doorknob.

"Chloe?" I called. She didn't answer.

BY THE END OF THE WEEK, we were all climbing the walls. Chloe seemed to have given up on spells involving the mice, instead meeting Joe in the garden early each morning to practice growing plants. I was glad there was no further errant magic, but the utter tedium of long days with no classes was almost worse. Sammy said her power didn't manifest in a way we could practice, and I was too scared to unleash mine beyond what I had to.

Our parents set up a common room for us, next to Chloe's and my bedrooms, but the space was dull. We lounged on old couches that smelt of dust and sadness, the blank white walls looming as if they would topple down on us like dominoes. I'd taken to reading one of the magical textbooks to stave off boredom – an encyclopaedia of spells. I was already up to F.

"What are we supposed to do now?" Joe asked, flopping down onto the couch beside Sammy. "You don't even have a TV."

"Who cares? At least we're not stuck in the classroom with that flighty old bat." Apparently, Chloe's repentant phase had lasted for less time than it took Arthur to recover.

Ben clicked his tongue. "Show some respect, Chloe. You could have killed her."

Chloe rolled her eyes. "Give off, she'll be fine. Look at Arthur and Joe. She was being dramatic."

I frowned. Dramatic didn't seem like Miss Caraway's style. I had a feeling her image was carefully curated – that floaty dress against the booming power of her voice. It was designed to surprise, to draw attention. There was no way she would give up that powerful image for the sake of feigning sickness.

"Forget about what happened. Joe's right – we should do something fun." Arthur practically jiggled as he spoke. "We have the whole night to ourselves."

Mum and Dad had gone to a function, dragging themselves away from their lurking watch over us after eliciting promises we wouldn't try any magic while they were away. They may as well have written a sign saying: "we're going out – start the explosions after 8 PM!"

It was all very well for Arthur to say we had the evening to ourselves, but there was nothing exciting for us to do. I almost suggested a board game, but that would have had Chloe rolling her eyes so far back she'd do herself damage.

"So, what do you do for fun around here?" Sammy asked.

Joe raised his eyebrows. "I think you're looking at it."

Chloe's cheeks turned pink at that. "We can head into town," she said. "We could see a movie or..." She frowned, as she scrambled for anything remotely interesting. Her eyes flicked towards Joe. "We could... Actually..." Chloe's face brightened. "I've got a friend who could probably get us some beer."

Ben frowned. "Oh, really? Who's this friend?"

"No one you know." Chloe tossed her hair, a smirk on her lips, and Ben's frown deepened.

Joe watched Chloe, his eyes narrowing, but the hint of a smile played at the corners of his mouth. "That doesn't sound too bad. I'm in – we're in, right Sammy?"

Sammy hesitated. She looked from Joe to Chloe, but Arthur cut in before she could say anything. "I'm in," he said. He got up and moved towards the door almost as if he would lead the way.

Drinking did not appeal to me – I'd probably just make a fool of myself – but I didn't want to be the only one left behind. "Yeah, I'm in too," I said.

"No." Ben shook his head. "No way, Urse."

Chloe scoffed. "Who said you were invited, squirt?"

"If you're all going, then I'm going." I hated how petulant that made me sound. Chloe glared at me, like I'd threatened to tell Mum and Dad if they left me. I wouldn't have done that, but it was tempting to say it if it would make Chloe include me.

"Sure," Arthur said, as if he had any authority in the situation. "Of course Ursula can come." He grabbed my hand, pulling me up beside him. I stumbled with the sudden movement, and his fingers tightened on mine, steadying me.

"No, she can't." Chloe crossed her arms.

I stared at Ben, giving him my best pleading look. He stared back, and for a moment, it seemed like he might relent. But then he shook his head.

"No, little mouse. I think you should sit this one out."

Behind him, Joe sniggered. I could have killed Ben for using that nickname. It wasn't fair. I was only a year younger than Arthur, but they were treating me like a baby.

"All right, it's settled. The rest of you…" Chloe's gaze fell on Arthur. She opened her mouth as if to protest him going too, but my brother slung his arm around Arthur's shoulder.

"Perhaps this will be a good geminus-bonding exercise," he said.

Arthur glanced at me. "If Ursula's not going…"

"It's fine," I said. "I don't like beer, anyway."

Chloe scoffed, knowing full well I'd never tried it.

"See you later, little mouse," Joe said, winking at me.

My cheeks flamed. Ben ruffled my hair, probably in a lame attempt at an apology, but all it did was annoy me more.

Joe stopped in the doorway. "You coming?"

I glanced up, ready to glare at him for making fun of me, but his eyes were on Sammy, who hadn't moved from her spot on the couch. She hesitated, looking at me. I shook my head. She couldn't hang back out of pity; that was humiliating.

"I'm going to stay with Ursula," she said finally. "If it's a geminus bonding thing, I should probably…"

"Seriously?" Joe frowned. Behind it, there was something else though… a hitch in his voice that almost sounded like he was hurt.

She swallowed and looked down. "It's not like I can drink anyway."

It got weirdly quiet in the room. We all had this stupid fascination with Sammy's pregnancy, but in a lot of ways, it wasn't real to the rest of us – just something to gossip and speculate on. Suddenly, it was almost as if the baby was already here, judging us for wanting to feed it beer.

"You could still come," Joe said. "You don't have to—"

"I'll see you all later." There was something final in Sammy's tone. Joe just stood there, staring at her. I felt like I'd watched an entire argument play out with only half the words spoken aloud.

"Fine. Suit yourself." Joe looked away, his expression dark.

Chloe slipped her arm through his and pulled him towards the door. "Don't worry. I'm sure we'll still have fun without them."

I shook my head at my sister's callousness. She smirked in response.

"Come on," Sammy said to me, once the others had gone. "We don't need them. We should do something fun ourselves."

It was sweet of her, but the idea felt forced. "You don't have to do that. You don't have to stay either. If you want to go with them—"

"I don't," she said firmly. "Even if you weren't staying back, I wouldn't have gone." She shook her head, then flicked her hands as if she was brushing off the others and their night out. "I mean it; let's do something fun. Let's... I don't know... Let's have a picnic. You can show me around the grounds."

I frowned. I could just imagine Chloe laughing at us if I told her we'd had a picnic, but it couldn't be worse than sitting on these lumpy couches, listening to the never-ending hammer beats. "Okay," I said begrudgingly, then I softened. "Actually, there is somewhere cool I could take you. It's not far – still on the grounds – but no one else knows about it."

Sammy's smile widened, lighting her face. "That sounds perfect." She took my hand, though I had a feeling it was mostly because she needed help getting off the couch. "Don't tell anyone, but I have a secret stash of chocolate," she said. "Not even Joe knows where I keep it."

I smiled at being let in on the secret. I didn't have the heart to tell her I wasn't that big a chocolate fan. "We could make chocolate strawberries," I said instead.

WE MELTED A COUPLE of Sammy's chocolate bars on the kitchen stove, tempering them ready to coat the berries. I would take Sammy up onto the roof of the old disused barn. It didn't sound that impressive, but the view from up there spread out across the hills and the sky. When I was little, I'd wanted my parents to build me a treehouse. They never did, but I'd figured out how to get up onto the roof of the barn, and that was almost as good. The best part was neither Ben nor Chloe knew about it.

Sammy pilfered a few other treats from the pantry, packing them all up in a Tupperware container. It wasn't a picnic basket, but it would do. We let the strawberries set, then headed out into the garden.

"Doesn't it give you the creeps, having all these people wandering around your house all the time?"

"Huh?" I glanced up. Sammy nodded to a group of workers milling around the grounds, finally having laid down their hammers for the night. I shrugged. "I guess I'm used to it. They've been here for a while."

"They're so strange though. They almost don't seem human."

Zombies, I thought again. Now that they were off duty, it was even worse. Without my dad giving orders, they just drifted across the lawn, eyes glazed.

"I think my dad is using magic on them." As soon as the words were out of my mouth, I wanted to pluck them back out of the air.

Sammy shivered. "He wouldn't do that to us, would he?"

I swallowed, unable to give the answer I knew I should. Sammy studied my face for a moment, her own expression unreadable. I couldn't hold her eye. Memories of Dad forcing Chloe and Ben to fight flashed through my mind. He'd never really hurt them, though, would he? It was just about making their magic better.

Sammy squeezed my hand, drawing my attention back to her. "Where's the spot you wanted to show me?"

I forced a smile, grateful for the distraction. "This way."

I pulled Sammy over to the tree beside the barn. The wide branches stretched up over the roof, solid... stable. I rested a hand on the bark, and the tree seemed to press back against me in welcome.

On the far side of the lawn, the workers had given up on milling around and now sat in the grass, like they were joining us in their own foodless picnic.

Sammy looked from me to the tree, frowning. "You're not expecting me to climb that, are you?" Her hands tightened over her belly.

I laughed. "No, of course not. It's just where I hide the key." I crouched down, retrieving the key from the roots of the tree. I unlocked the side door of the barn, and led Sammy to the narrow staircase leading up to the roof. Sammy looked almost as dubious about climbing the steps as she had about the tree.

"I won't let you fall," I told her. "I promise."

She took a long breath, letting it out slowly through her lips. "I trust you," she said finally. "You better catch me and bub if I slip, though." She laughed as she said it, but I nodded, making the promise seriously.

I walked up first with the food, opening the trapdoor to the roof, then came back to help Sammy. She gripped my arm tighter than I was expecting, fear turning her fingers into wiry claws. I guess it was a bit daunting with no handrail and one side of the stairs open to the barn. But still... she trusted me enough to do this. I wasn't going to take that lightly.

"I've got you," I told her.

She took a breath and then nodded. We took the steps one at a time. I gripped her tightly, pulling her up partly with magic and partly with sheer strength. Perhaps it had been insensitive of me to suggest this. I hadn't thought how hard it would be for her, with the baby weighing heavily on her. By the time we reached the roof, her breath came in sharp, ragged gasps. She lay back on the corrugated iron, laughing, letting the heavy rise and fall of her chest slow, and I flopped back too.

"Oof. That's my exercise for the week," she said.

From up here, we could see all of the stars, far enough away from the lights of the house for the sky to really show its magic. The bright dots danced against the inky darkness as if performing just for us.

"Wow," she said softly, not letting her voice disturb the night. "This is beautiful."

If I'd brought Chloe up here, she would have scoffed, even if she thought it was pretty. I settled back next to Sammy, letting the soft night sounds wash over us.

"You're good at protective magic, aren't you?" Sammy asked.

I shrugged. "I guess."

"You are. You helped Arthur the other day when the rest of us couldn't even touch him."

"*We* helped Arthur the other day." I couldn't have done it if Sammy hadn't taken my hand. I still wasn't entirely sure *what* we had done, but I knew it hadn't been me alone.

Sammy fell quiet, her earlier laughter completely disappearing. "I guess that's this geminus thing they keep talking about." Her voice was low, making it hard to judge how she felt about it. I wasn't sure either. Sammy's magic had made me feel stronger, but I wasn't sure I wanted to have to hold someone's hand every time I used my power.

"You knew it was going to happen, didn't you?"

Sammy looked up at me, her gaze sharp. I swallowed, not wanting to back down now I'd said it. "That bit Chloe read out from your notebook – you'd written about what was going to happen."

Sammy nodded slowly. "Sometimes, I write things, but—"

"Then why didn't you try to stop it? How could you let them get hurt?"

Sammy hesitated, then slipped her hand inside her jacket. She pulled her notebook from inside the lining. "Here."

I took the notebook from her, but I didn't open it. Suddenly, I wasn't sure if I wanted answers to any of my questions.

Sammy bit her lip, and nodded, gesturing towards the book. "Read it."

I opened the book. Pages of scrawling words greeted me. I flicked through them. Names jumped out at me – my own, Chloe's and Ben's – but each time I tried to focus on the words around them, they moved, letters shifting and changing under my gaze.

She took the book back. "I don't remember writing it. I can only read bits when it's important," Sammy said quietly. "Until then, it's gibberish."

So that's what Chloe meant about Sammy writing in code. "But Chloe and Ben both read it."

Sammy nodded. "I think the magic was trying to stop Chloe from hurting the others. That must be why she found my book in the first place."

I shivered, cold suddenly. I knew magic could influence things – nudge people in a different direction or sway outcomes, but this was a different kind of power than any I'd witnessed before. "You've written a lot about us," I said.

Sammy's eyelashes flickered. "Yes."

Something curdled in my stomach. She'd read some of it, I was sure of it. I drew breath, ready to ask her if there was something she knew, ready to beg her to let me read what she had written, but a scrabbling sound cut me off.

Sammy grabbed my hand, her nails biting into my skin. We both looked towards the trapdoor where we'd just climbed up.

"There you are." Arthur's head appeared. He grinned at us.

Sammy let out a nervous laugh. "Oh, it's you."

I couldn't tell from her tone whether she was happy to see him or just relieved he wasn't someone worse. She moved back across the roof so he could climb out. I frowned. There was so much more I wanted to know about her prophecies. How could she be sure she was just predicting things and not causing them to happen?

"How did you find us?" Sammy asked.

Arthur shrugged. "Magic, of course. Ooo, strawberries." He dove into the Tupperware container, grabbing two of the chocolate berries, and then settled himself beside me.

"Why did you come back?"

Arthur shifted uncomfortably. His knee brushed mine as he did, but he didn't move away. "They got drunk really quickly. Then they were using magic on people, and..." He trailed off and glanced at me, falling silent.

That told me everything I needed to know. When he said "they" were using magic on people, he really meant Chloe.

"I bet Joe was egging them on." Sammy picked at some lint on her skirt. She didn't look up at either of us.

"Yeah, he was." Arthur didn't seem to register her mood. "The two of them started letting off fireworks, but then that turned into explosions and the whole thing got out of control. Joe seems like kind of a loose cannon. I don't know if I want to be around him, to be honest."

I nudged Arthur in the side, and he glanced up at me. I looked meaningfully at Sammy, especially her stomach. She still worried at the lint on her top. If she kept going any longer, she would pull a hole in the fabric. She chewed on her lip, perhaps trying to tear that too.

"I mean, it was fine," Arthur said quickly, his voice too high to be believable. "They were just having fun, I guess."

"Fun at other people's expense." Sammy flopped back on the roof, staring up at the stars. I leaned back with her, looking up, and after a second, Arthur joined us.

"He's not a bad guy," Sammy said. "He's actually a really *good* guy, I love him a lot. But it's just..."

I think I knew what she meant. People could get influenced by magic really easily, get carried away with it. Ben could be like that. Sometimes I had doubts about my sister's morality, but it wasn't like that with Ben. He just got excited and took his magic too far. I could see the same thing might be happening with Joe.

Sammy closed her eyes, resting her arm across her forehead. We let the silence hang damply over us for a moment.

"What type of magic do you have, Arthur?" I asked, breaking it.

Arthur blinked at the change of subject and looked towards me. I stared back at him, hoping he got the hint that we were done talking about Joe and my sister.

"I can do a little bit of everything," he said finally. He said it shyly, as if he wasn't all that sure in his own abilities. Somehow, that made me certain he was actually very good. Funny how things worked like that.

"That sounds cool," I said.

We both looked at Sammy, but she didn't open her eyes. Part of me resented Arthur for that. I'd been enjoying talking to Sammy alone. It reminded me of when Chloe and I were younger, and we used to stay up talking, long after Mum and Dad thought we had gone to bed.

"You two can obviously do some powerful stuff. I felt when you stopped that magic in the classroom."

I was surprised he'd felt anything, given how much it had been affecting him. An image flashed through my mind, and my thoughts scrambled after it, trying to catch hold.

"Did either of you see a rune?" I asked. With everything else that had happened, I'd forgotten about the brief spark of light I'd seen marking the rune on the inside of my eyelids, but suddenly it felt important.

Arthur frowned. "Like the ones on the floor?"

I shook my head. "No, it flashed in the air when the light flared." Just like the one that had sparked when Chloe led the mice. "You saw it, right?" I turned to Sammy.

She shook her head. "I don't think so."

Arthur looked down at his hands, rubbing them gently together, perhaps remembering the way his skin had turned black and withered. Even in the dark, I could see him shiver.

Sammy reached out, gently squeezing Arthur's hand. "Whatever it was, it's gone now." She smiled, but it didn't light her face the way it normally would.

"Can you see the geminus connections?" I asked. I reached out as I spoke, grabbing hold of the cord of magic between me and Sammy. It sparked as I made contact, a small wave of power rippling off it. The others reeled back, feeling the energy even if they couldn't see it.

Sammy touched her stomach, where the cord connected to her. "Woah... that was strong."

Arthur prodded the air in front of him, as if feeling for his connection to Ben. He missed it by a good twenty centimetres. That was probably a good thing.

"You must see magic in ways we can't," Sammy told me. Her voice dropped low again, and I couldn't help feeling she saw some significance in that. I lay back, retraining my focus on the night sky. It didn't look quite so beautiful now.

Arthur seemed to register the heavy mood that had fallen over me and Sammy. He pointed out the constellations above us, perhaps as a way to distract us, but I found I couldn't concentrate on his words. Instead of faraway celestial lights, I saw runes flashing in my mind.

The rune in the classroom had been significant, I was sure of it. I'd been thinking of what happened as an accident – another example of Chloe's overenthusiastic magic use, but doubt crept in now. What if she had known exactly what she was doing?

I shook my head, brushing the thought away. My sister wasn't like that. She was self-absorbed sometimes, and a bit mean, but she never set out to actually hurt anyone, did she? Suddenly, I wasn't sure of the answer. The world was tipping underneath me, and if I wasn't careful, my sister might lead me right off the edge.

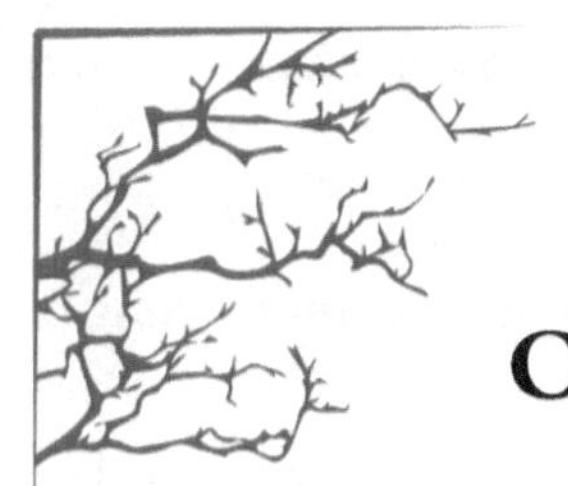

Chapter Five

S ammy looked about ready to collapse by the time we got back to the dormitory floor. She gave us each a hug, which made me stiffen, not used to physical affection from... well, anyone except my mother.

Arthur walked down the hallway with me. "I'm sorry Ben and Chloe didn't let you come with us tonight."

"I don't care," I said automatically, then I realised I actually meant it. I'd felt left out before, but I'd had a better time here with Sammy and Arthur than I would have had in town.

"I'm glad I came back," Arthur said. "It was fun getting to know you and Sammy."

"I'm glad you did too." I was surprised to find I meant that as well.

Arthur opened the door to the stairs and light poured through. He turned towards me, and I saw him clearly for the first time all night, our conversations having been sheltered in darkness. A dark swirl marked his cheek.

"You've got something on your face," I said. "It looks like..." My stomach dropped. It looked like ash, but that wasn't what made me pause. The mark curved into the shape of a rune.

I shook my head, trying to clear it. It couldn't be. The mark didn't mean anything. It *couldn't* mean anything.

Arthur brushed his cheek. "I think that's from the fireworks... and the fire."

The weight in my stomach grew. "There was another fire?"

"Oh, it was just an accident. They got it under control quickly."

Accident or not, Chloe hadn't learnt anything from the last time. I turned towards the old library, almost against my will. The lines of ash seemed to scream a warning, forcing me back.

"I have to go," I blurted out.

Arthur blinked, his eyelashes fluttering.

"Sleep," I said. "I need to sleep."

Arthur's gaze relaxed, releasing me from its intensity. "Yeah, me too." He smiled and touched my arm gently. "Dream well, Ursula."

I forced myself to keep a slow, steady pace on the first few steps, breaking into a run only once I heard the bottom stairwell door close. The pounding of my heartbeat turned to pulsing in my ears, reminding me of the hammers. Always the hammers; I couldn't escape them.

I closed the top stairwell door behind me, leaning against it. It was irrational, right? My fear had no base. Magical accidents happened; the library didn't need to fill me with all this dread... *my sister* didn't need to fill me with all this dread. Arthur would be fine. He had to be.

I let out a slow breath and opened my eyes.

Ben and Chloe weren't back yet, their rooms sitting empty in darkness. My exhales came a little easier at that. My fear may have been irrational, but I still didn't want to face my sister tonight.

A light came from down the corridor – my parents' room. I hesitated, straining to hear if they were home.

A voice floated towards me. "There's something wrong."

I frowned. That was Miss Caraway. What was she doing in Mum's room? I edged my way along the corridor, listening.

Her pacing figure moved back and forth across Mum's doorway. "None of their powers are as strong as they should be. *My* power isn't as strong as it should be."

Nausea rolled in my stomach. I thought I'd got away with hiding my magic, but it sounded like Miss Caraway had noticed. Except... she wasn't just talking about me.

None of their powers are as strong as they should be... How much magic was she expecting us to have?

An image of those dark veins creeping up her arms flashed through my head. My sister had taken some of her power – some of Joe's and Arthur's too – but that wasn't permanent, right? They had regained it once Chloe stopped, surely.

I swallowed. Unless Chloe had done irrevocable damage to them. I shuffled forward, hoping to get a glimpse of Miss Caraway's arms now.

"I know, but..." Mum stopped suddenly, and so did Miss Caraway. Everything went quiet – too quiet – that hollow, stretching sort of silence when someone is listening. I froze with them, willing myself to turn to stone.

"Ursula?" Mum called.

Damn. I hadn't made a sound, had I? But somehow they still knew I was there. I hesitated, then padded my way down the corridor.

The room was lit just from Mum's bedside lamp. It cast a warm glow, creating a cosy atmosphere. Miss Caraway and

Mum both smiled as I appeared in the doorway. There was no sign of the worry I'd heard in their voices just before, except for the fact that Miss Caraway's smile didn't reach her eyes.

"Hello, dear," she said.

"Hi..." I said. "You look better."

Miss Caraway raised her eyebrows, and I blushed, but then she nodded. "Thank you. I feel better."

"Where's Dad?" I asked.

Mum frowned. "He had some things to finish up down-stairs."

I thought of the zombie-like workers drifting over the lawn, waiting for him to return, and my stomach curdled once more. Would he gather them up again, forcing them to pick up tools and trudge after him until the early hours of the morning?

Miss Caraway studied my face, as if she saw some trace of what I was thinking. "I was just about to head off," she said. "Why don't you walk with me, Ursula?"

I glanced at Mum. They'd been mid-argument just moments before; it hadn't sounded like she'd been about to leave.

Mum chewed on her lip, her eyes flicking between me and Miss Caraway. "Yes, go on, love," she said finally. Then she looked back at Miss Caraway. "We'll finish this tomorrow."

There was an urgency in Mum's voice that made me want to run to her, but Miss Caraway's hand clamped down on my shoulder before I could object. I stared back at Mum, as Miss Caraway guided me away. Mum looked so small, suddenly. Had she always been that thin, or had creating a school carved pieces of her away along with parts of the building?

"How are you finding learning magic, Ursula?" Miss Car-away asked.

I turned back to face her, blinking as I tried to refocus. How was I supposed to answer that? We'd had only half a magic lesson before everything had gone wrong.

"It's okay," I said finally. *It's scary*, was the real answer. Scary and confusing.

The cosy feeling of Mum's room dropped away the further we got down the dark corridor. Shadows seemed to move around us, closing in. They were just like the ash outside the library, creeping closer and closer. Even worse, that hollow, empty feeling was coming with them.

Miss Caraway stopped and turned towards me. "Trust your magic, Ursula. It's stronger than you realise."

I didn't know what to say to that either. I made myself nod, and she frowned slightly. She studied my face for a moment longer, then touched my shoulder gently. "Goodnight, dear."

I forced myself not to shrink from her. "Goodnight, Miss Caraway."

I watched her walk to the stairs. The shadows shifted away from her, almost as if she could bend the light to her will. Or, more likely, they weren't just shadows, and they knew to run from her power. Could she feel it too? That sense of something bad coming? Sammy had said I saw magic in ways the others didn't, but Miss Caraway had seen something too, I was sure of it.

I WOKE TO THE SOUND of voices, then a sharp knock on my door. I dragged myself up, groggily, and opened it. Miss Caraway stood in the corridor, Sammy beside her.

"Good, you're awake. Can Samantha share your room for a while?" Miss Caraway didn't wait for me to answer. She pushed Sammy forward, closing the door behind her. We heard the click of it locking... except I didn't have a lock on my door. I tried the handle, but it was stuck fast, magic sealing us in here.

Sammy turned to me. Her face blanched pale, and she pulled her robe tightly over her stomach as if she could protect the baby with her grip alone. Lines of blue ink marked her hands; she'd been writing again.

"What's going on? What time is it even?"

"It's just after 4 AM." Sammy swallowed, a shiver working its way up her body. I took her hand, pulling her towards the bed. We sat down cross-legged, facing each other. "There's something wrong with Arthur," she said.

My hand flew to my mouth automatically. Though I'd tried to convince myself I was imagining it, I'd felt something was wrong last night – a growing dread that something was going to happen. I'd seen the rune drawn in ash on Arthur's cheek, but I hadn't done anything. I hadn't even wiped it off for him; I just left him to sort it alone.

"We have to help him."

Sammy shook her head. "We can't. They've closed off the whole floor. Joe's in Ben's room. There are workers stationed at the doors, not to mention the runes your mum laid."

"What happened? What's wrong with Arthur?"

"They say he's sick, but he's not. It's like all of his power is being sucked out of him. He stumbled into my room, and he was so hot – burning – but so, so pale."

My own forehead burned, a restless feverishness coming over me.

"It's the magic," Sammy told me firmly. "It's doing something strange, like it's being drawn out of everything, not just him. I don't know, can't you feel it? The wrongness of it?"

Out of the corners of my eyes, I saw black shadows stretching across the room; fingers of ashy darkness reaching for me. They disappeared when I looked directly at them.

"We need to tell someone," Sammy said. "Your parents?"

I swallowed, nausea building in my throat. I loved my mum, but she had looked so frail last night. Would she help us if we asked? *Could* she even help? And my dad...

"I don't know if we can trust them." My voice cracked on the words. They felt like a betrayal to my family.

Sammy's eyes went wide. "What do you mean?"

Where did I start? Sammy was right, there was something wrong with the magic, but how did I explain that I thought it might be my sister causing it? How could I tell her that Chloe might have hurt Joe – tried to drain his magic for her own use – on purpose?

Sammy squeezed my hand. "Please, Ursula... I need to know."

I closed my eyes. She was my geminus pair. If anyone could help, it would be her. "That rune I saw, when Chloe hurt Joe – I saw it again."

"When?"

"Chloe did a spell with some mice. She was controlling them."

Sammy's hand flew to her mouth. "And you think that's what she was trying to do to Joe?"

"Maybe... I don't know. I think it's what my dad is doing to the workers." I shook my head. My family had always pulled energy from plants and other objects to fuel their magic, but never to this scale. I'd never seen them take power from people before.

Sammy closed her eyes. She shook her head slowly back and forth. She didn't ask for more details, but it was like she was plucking them from the air around us, filling in the blanks of all the things I couldn't bear to say aloud. I knew my dad misused magic, gaining money and status because of it. But this was something even darker.

"I don't think Chloe's doing this on purpose," I said quietly. "I think the magic is influencing her – taking control."

"That's almost worse."

Was my sister really all that bad? If Dad hadn't pushed her to fight Ben, she never would have cared how strong her power was.

Suddenly Sammy opened her eyes and pulled her notebook from inside her robe. She whipped through the pages, nearly tearing them as she flung them back.

"What is it? Did you write something?"

She shook her head. "I don't know, it just sounds familiar." Something caught her eye, and she stilled, reading. I peered over her shoulder, but the words remained gibberish to me. She murmured to herself, then pressed her lips together, thinking. She closed the book, her focus landing back on me.

"If we can't trust your parents, then who can we talk to?" she asked.

I studied her face. Her cheeks were drawn, worry changing her features in the short time she had been here. Miss Caraway had said that none of our powers were as strong as they should be. I hoped that didn't mean Chloe was draining Sammy too.

An even more uncomfortable thought occurred to me then – was Chloe draining *my* power? Would I be able to tell if my sister was leaching off me, taking away my magic?

"Miss Caraway," I said finally. "She'll help us."

"You're sure?"

I nodded. "She knows something is wrong; she can feel it too, I'm sure of it."

"Okay, that's a start. Anyone else?"

"Ben," I said, though my voice didn't come out with as much conviction. Would he listen to me, or would he dismiss me with a pat on the head, calling me "little mouse"?

Sammy didn't answer, perhaps having the same doubts I was.

"What about Joe?" I asked. I didn't know if I trusted Sammy's boyfriend, but he was Chloe's geminus pair. Maybe he could help her. We had to at least try.

Sammy nodded slowly. "I'll talk to him. Your magic is the strongest, so you should go help Arthur."

"But the door's locked."

"Don't worry about that. We can break it."

She said that so certainly, but I glanced at the door, dubious. Breaking through a normal lock was one thing, but I had no idea where to start with Miss Caraway's magical one.

Even if we weren't trapped in here, I had another issue with Sammy's plan – one that I didn't want to voice. I was scared of going downstairs alone.

Sammy studied my face, seeming to read some of what I was thinking. "Can you put your magic into objects?" she asked. "Protection, I mean, like when you kept me from falling down the barn stairs?"

"I don't know. What type of objects?"

She slipped one of the bracelets from her wrist. "This?"

I took the silver band. If I could add the magic to it, it would double my natural protective magic... but that was a very big if. Sammy had already told me she couldn't do this kind of magic – that hers was confined to writing. If we tried to work this spell, it would all be on me.

I glanced at Sammy's notebook. Her magic manifested as writing, but maybe she had written *this*. She mentioned the bracelet like she'd just thought of it, but the steadiness of her gaze told me different. She'd read something important in her notebook just now, I was sure of it. Maybe she wasn't coming up with the idea here, in the moment, but following a plan her unconscious self had left for her.

I reached for her hands, and she gripped mine. "We can try," I said.

Sammy nodded, then closed her eyes. I felt her magic reach out. It twisted around mine, glimpses of it flickering at the edges of my vision. My power was strong, but unpractised. A heavy tiredness pressed me down towards the mattress, and my hands shook with the effort, but I kept going. I had to. I could feel the danger around us building – the "wrongness" as Sammy called it.

I forced magic into the metal, driving power right down into its core.

"That's it," Sammy whispered. "Keep going." She slipped the other bracelets from her wrist, laying them out on the bedspread. I pushed magic into all of them until they hummed with it, shimmering with supernatural strength.

This was stronger than anything I could have done alone. I looked up at Sammy, and she nodded, pleased with what we'd created. Together, we might just protect the others, and if we were lucky, we might even be able to protect Chloe from herself.

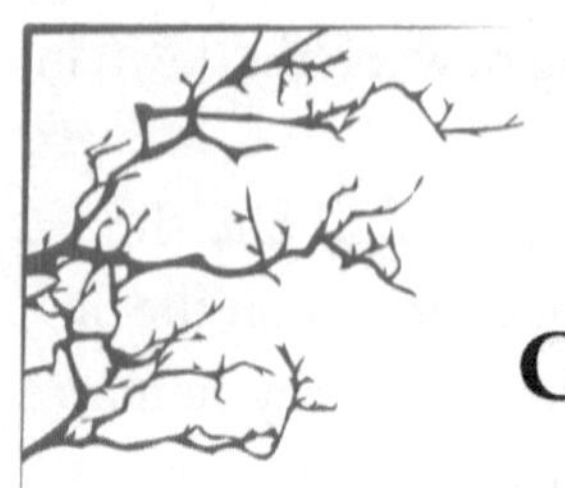

Chapter Six

The stack of bracelets clicked against each other as I walked down the stairs. I clasped a hand over the top to silence them. Sammy had only taken one, giving me the rest. They didn't make me feel any safer about going downstairs, but Sammy was right; I had to be the one to help Arthur.

The halls were quiet, and dimly lit, as the sun outside the window inched up above the hills. A worker stood in the stairwell in front of the dormitory door, his face in shadow. I remembered Sammy's words about the whole floor being closed off, guards posted at the doors. I hesitated, then walked towards him.

"I want to see Arthur," I said, making my voice as firm as I could muster.

He blinked, his eyelids fluttering to show he'd heard, but he didn't answer. I almost turned back right then, but Miss Caraway's voice echoed in my mind. *Your magic is stronger than you realise.*

"I'm going to go see him," I told him, almost as firmly. Then: "Okay?" Not at all firm now – weak and pleading – but I had said the words. That was something.

The man still didn't respond. His eyes shone with a glassy glaze, and he swayed ever so slightly. What was I doing, trying to reason with zombies? I pushed past him, half expecting him to reach out an arm to stop me, but no barrier came down, and no clutching hand held me back. He blinked as I touched him, though, his eyes clearing just a little.

Good. Perhaps he would snap out of it and stop letting my dad siphon power off him. I let the door close behind me and padded down the corridor to Arthur's room. My feet tingled as I crossed the rune line – my own protective magic seeming to scan me and assess whether it would let me pass.

"It's me," I whispered, half to Arthur, half to the line of power defending the entrance. The tingling swelled to humming, vibrating up my legs. I turned Arthur's doorhandle, quietly pleased that the magic recognised me.

Arthur's room was warm – too warm. A wave of heat hit me as soon as I crossed the threshold, coming from Arthur himself.

"Arthur?" I whispered.

He didn't stir. Bright spots of red bloomed in his cheeks, but the rest of his face was unnaturally pale. I could feel a rush of energy flowing away from him, just like it had in the classroom when he touched Joe.

I pulled the strongest bracelet from my wrist, slipping it over his hand. "This will protect you," I said.

Power thrummed from it. I felt it swelling out from the jewellery, wrapping Arthur in a thin layer of protective magic. But he didn't wake. His hand flopped back onto the bedspread as soon as I let go of it, the bracelet dangling.

Energy leached out of him. If I followed the thread of it, I was sure I'd find my selfish sister at the other end, or worse, my father, who was well old enough to know better.

"You have to fight back, Arthur," I told him.

No runes marked his flushed cheeks now, but I rubbed them with the heel of my palm anyway, as if I could ward off the invisible symbol. "Come on, Arthur! Wake up."

Something tingled against my skin, and I gasped, jerking my hand away. Black streaks of ash lined my palm, coming from his cheek. I scrubbed at his face. "Wake up!" I told him fiercely. "You have to wake up!"

The bracelet was useless. All the magic we had poured into it, yet it did nothing. Anger built inside me, and with it heat. Why had Sammy's stupid book told her to waste that magic when it didn't even work? I hated this!

I reached for his hand, squeezing it. I wanted to say something reassuring, promise him I would figure out how to stop the magic draining from him, but there was only one way to make this stop for good, and that was at the source.

"I'm going to fix this," I told him. "I promise."

He didn't open his eyes, and if anything, he just got paler. I gave his hand one last fierce squeeze, then turned and ran from the room.

The worker outside the door glared at me as I passed him, finally showing some independent thought. I didn't wait for him to yell at me – to ask what I was doing on the closed floor. I just kept running, praying he wouldn't leave his post to chase me.

I found Joe and Chloe down at the bottom of the garden, where they practised each morning. Joe had covered every inch of one of the walls in vines. It was impressive really, though the strength of his magic scared me. He reminded me of Chloe, in a way. Unpredictable – nice one minute, playing with dangerous spells the next.

"I need to talk to you," I told Chloe.

She glanced my way, then back at Joe's ivy wall. "We're busy, squirt. Why don't you go bug Sammy?"

I wavered, half ready to turn away. A part of me wanted to give up – to find Ben or Miss Caraway and tell them how dangerous Chloe's magic had become. But I couldn't do that to her. She was my sister; I had to at least give her a chance to get it back under control first.

"Please, Chloe. It's important!"

She let out an exaggerated breath. Her hair was loose, falling in messy waves around her shoulders. It made her look younger; it made her look more like me.

She stared at me for a moment, then glanced up at the vine wall. "How fast can you make them grow?" she asked Joe.

Joe grinned. "Fast as you want, baby." He waggled his eyebrows.

"Chloe, please!" I stomped my foot like a little kid. "This is serious! Arthur's really sick."

"Okay, okay!" Chloe grabbed my shoulders, pushing me towards the wall. "Stand here, and we can talk."

I shook my head. "Your magic is out of control. I know you've been—"

"Hold your hands out to the sides." Chloe raised my arms, moving me like a mannequin. She stepped back, beckoning to Joe. He looked from her to me, a puzzled grin on his face.

"What are you doing?" Panic rose in my chest. I dropped my arms, moving to step away from the wall, but she held up a hand for me to stay.

"I want to try something."

"But—"

"You say my magic is out of control, well this is how I learn to manage it." She fixed me with a stare. Her lips curled into a smile, but there was a challenge in her expression.

Was this an ultimatum? Would she leave Arthur alone if I helped her with this spell? Reluctantly, I stepped back against the wall, lifting my hands to the sides. Joe grinned. Apparently, he didn't even need to know what Chloe's idea was to think it was a good one.

"Can you make them grow?" she asked him.

My heart hammered. "Wait, what are you going to do?"

A slithering sound came from behind me. Chloe moved towards me, raising her hand. Vines shot out from the wall, wrapping around my arms. I screamed, jerking away, but they held me fast. "Chloe!"

The vines circled my limbs, tighter and tighter. Suddenly, they lurched up, taking me with them. I let out a shriek.

"It's working!" Chloe burst into giggles.

Joe's mouth fell open. "Woah," he said. "I never thought of doing that!"

I drew breath, ready to shriek again, but the vines didn't drop me. They held me securely in the air.

"See?" Chloe called. "I can control my magic when I want to. Do you want to go higher?"

The little gleam in her eye told me she was going to send me higher anyway. Joe closed his eyes, pushing the vines to grow faster. Chloe whispered something, directing them up, and I shot further into the air. I shrieked again.

"Chloe!" Ben's voice rang out from across the garden. I turned my head to see him and Sammy racing towards us.

"What are you doing!?" Ben grabbed Chloe's arm and the vines loosened. I gasped, throwing out a lasso of magic to anchor myself.

Chloe shook him off. "Relax. Ursula's having fun."

Fun was an exaggeration, but I was okay, and the more energy Chloe focused on me, the less she would have available to drain Arthur. Ben peered up at me, and I raised my hand, giving him a thumbs up.

"You sure you're okay, Urse?" His narrowed eyes traced the lines of the vines supporting me. I nodded, though the movement made the vines shake.

"Sammy, you'll love this," Joe said. "You should try it after you have the baby."

She frowned. "I don't know. Are you sure Ursula's safe?" She stared up at me, chewing on her lip.

I found I couldn't quite meet her gaze. I should have updated her after I left Arthur's room. This wasn't what Sammy and I had agreed, but I still wanted a chance to talk to Chloe, to persuade her to reign her magic in. Ben stared at Chloe, his gaze hard. Had Sammy already told him everything? Something about the way he was looking at Chloe made me feel cold.

My sister's face darkened at Sammy's criticism. "Of course it's safe." She twisted her hand slightly, and the vines tightened around my raised thumb.

I gasped. "Don't, that hurts." Suddenly, the vines were growing faster, wrapping around me.

"Hey, stop that!" Ben shoved Joe's shoulder, but Joe shook his head. "I'm not doing anything. They shouldn't be growing anymore."

I looked back at Chloe, and her hand twisted again. "I can make them grow too," she said. Her breath came out in a puff. She curled her fingers, excitement lighting her face.

"Please, Chloe!" I gasped.

Something flashed in the air in front of her – a spark of light. Then the vines covered my face. One of them found its way into my mouth. I spat it out, a strange taste crossing my tongue. I tried to pull away, but foliage bound my hands. I squirmed, breaking the stalks, and I lost hold of my own magic. Suddenly, the only thing supporting me was the thin strings of leaves. Fleshy pops sounded as they snapped, straining under my weight. I opened my mouth to scream but vines poured into it.

"Oh my god, stop!" Ben scrambled up the wall towards me. The vines wrapped around him too. He grabbed my ankle and immediately vines bound around us like handcuffs. "God dammit, make it stop!"

"I don't know how!" Joe yelled. He joined Ben at the wall, ripping vines free. But they were growing faster and faster. I could barely breathe through the leaves wrapping around my face.

That strange taste filled my mouth again. Ash – that's what it was. The vines were withering, energy leaching out of them even as they grew.

Suddenly, Chloe shrieked, then there was a thud. The vines dropped away, and I fell. Joe and Ben tumbled backwards too, all of us landing in a heap.

Chloe lay on the ground, her face indignant. Sammy stood over her, her hands splayed out, as if she'd just shoved Chloe. It took me a moment to realise that's exactly what had happened.

Ben pulled me upright. "Are you okay, Ursula?"

The others crowded around me, and Sammy's hand slipped into mine, squeezing it.

"Yeah…" I started to say, but my voice sounded very far away. The vines – Joe and Chloe's spells – had dissolved, as had the magic I had been using to keep myself safe. Sammy's bracelets had fallen from my wrist, scattering in the grass. I reached for one, but my limbs felt heavy, almost as if I wasn't in control of them.

"You didn't have to push me!" Chloe got up, dusting herself off. "I would have figured out how to stop it." She glared at Sammy.

Sammy shook her head. "Oh yeah? When exactly? Ursula could have been hurt! And after what you did to Arthur—"

"What do you care? She's my sister, not yours."

Sparks appeared on the surface of my skin. They drifted out, floating away from me. I reached for one, but the magic slipped out of my grasp, no longer mine. I felt weak, suddenly. Dizzy. More sparks floated away, coming from my arms. They left black spots in their place. Black, ashy spots like my skin was burning.

"Are you okay, Ursula?" Sammy reached out to touch my arm.

I jerked away. "Don't!"

Her hand connected with one of the black spots. She gasped, flinching back. Then she shuddered, going rigid.

"Sammy!" Joe caught her as she fell. Her eyes went wide, her skin paling instantly.

"The ash!" I hissed. "She touched the ash!" But no one was listening to me. Chloe screamed something at Ben, her words incomprehensible.

"Help her, Ursula!" Joe yelled.

I scrambled to grab the bracelets, pushing as many as I could find onto her wrist. They felt like cheap, useless trinkets in my hands, the magic not strong enough to help anyone. Sammy's eyes rolled, trying to find mine. I felt Joe start something, some spell growing around her, and I added my power to his. Sammy's fingers inched out, reaching for my hand. I gripped hers, pouring all of my protective magic into her palm.

Sammy gasped and so did Joe. I shuddered, as I felt an icy rush of air inside her, just like I had with Arthur and Miss Caraway. But it was different this time – grittier and bitter tasting. Filled with ash.

And something else was different. This time it wasn't trying to pull me in.

"No," I whispered.

Sparks flowed from my skin, my magic drifting away. But the icy rush came from inside me. *I* was draining Sammy's magic, siphoning it through the geminus connection.

I clasped my free hand to my stomach, as if I could dam up the flow. Sparks appeared around my fist. I pulled my shirt up, revealing an ashy burn mark around my belly button. "No, no, no!"

The others stared at me, unable to see the magic the way I could; unable to see the damage I was causing. "Help!" I screamed, putting every ounce of magic I had left into the call. "Make it stop!"

The words echoed out, drawing every magical member of staff to us. They came running, bursting out of the doors of the house. Mum and Dad ran towards us. My mother took in the scene, shaking her head slowly. "What have you done?" she whispered.

Chloe opened her mouth to speak, but Mum didn't wait for an answer, turning to Sammy instead. She hovered over her as if afraid to touch her.

"It wasn't—" I started to say, but my father pushed me away.

"That's enough, Ursula!" he said. "Let go of her."

"It's coming from me!" I said, but no one was listening. My father gathered Sammy up in his arms, pushing both me and Joe away. In a blink, they were gone again, all of the adults disappearing, taking Sammy with them.

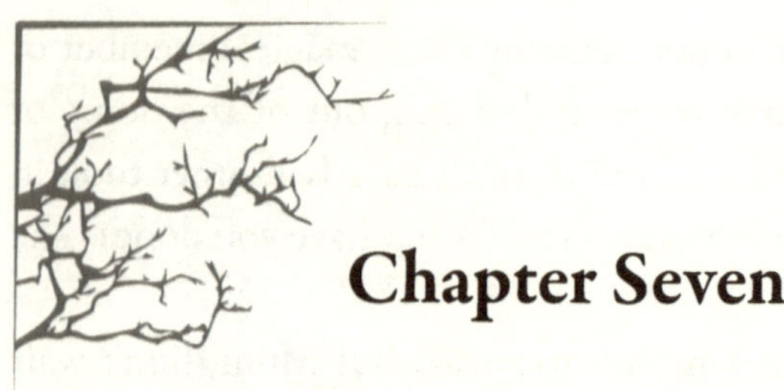

Chapter Seven

Sammy wasn't in her room. Joe grabbed her pillow, as if he thought he might find her hiding under it, then he hurled it across the room. "Where did they take her?" he screamed at me.

I shrank back, and Ben automatically stepped in front of me, hands raised protectively. Chloe put her arm around me, but I cringed at the touch.

"I don't know," I whispered. "They shouldn't have taken her away." *They should have let me help her.*

"There's a medical bay – there *will be* a medical bay," Ben said. "It's not finished but they might have taken her there."

"They'll be worried about the baby," Chloe added.

"Where is it?" Joe lurched towards the door, but Ben pressed a hand to his chest, stopping him.

"I'll go. They'll tell me more than they will you. I'll let you know anything I find out, okay?"

"But I need…" Joe wavered for a moment, the end of the sentence disappearing with his resolve. He sank down on the bed, clutching his head in his hands. "Please, just find out if she's okay? They both have to be okay."

Ben tilted his head towards the door, gesturing for me and Chloe to join him. Chloe's arm fell from my shoulders as we walked into the corridor. Ben shut the door, and he and Chloe rounded on each other.

"What the hell were you thinking?" he yelled at her. His eyes blazed, and he flung out a hand emphatically.

"Me? I wouldn't have had to if you hadn't—"

"What's going on?" Arthur appeared in his doorway.

I gasped. "You're awake!" I grabbed him, pulling him into a hug. He squeezed me back for a moment, then I pulled away to look at him. Dark hollows marked his cheeks, but he was up and standing unaided, so that had to be a good sign. "What happened?" I asked. "How are you better?"

He shook his head. "I don't know. I just woke up a few minutes ago."

A few minutes ago, as in at the same time Sammy collapsed? That couldn't be a coincidence.

"What's going on?" Arthur asked. "Why are you yelling?" He looked to Ben and Chloe. They just stared at each other, fury clouding their faces.

"Sammy's hurt," I said. "Like you and Miss Caraway."

Arthur's eyes flicked towards Chloe, but I shook my head. "It was my fault. Sammy touched my arm, and..." I gulped, tears shutting the words down.

Ben turned away from Chloe, blinking. "What? This wasn't your doing, little mouse."

I just shook my head. The sensation of the icy air rushing through me still chilled my core. I had drained Sammy's magic... Maybe it had been me all along.

"Ben's right," Chloe said, her voice strained. "It wasn't your fault, Urse." A silent conversation seemed to pass between my brother and sister, none of it accessible to me. Arthur looked between us, his brow creasing.

"I told Joe I'd find out what's happening," Ben said finally.

Chloe gave a sharp nod. "I'll go with you. We need to talk." She looked back at me, and her face softened. "It will be okay. I promise."

The fact that Chloe was trying to reassure me unnerved me more than anything else. Ben took hold of Chloe's arm, not altogether gently, and they set off down the corridor.

Arthur turned to me once they were gone. "What on earth is going on?"

I shook my head and took his hand, pulling him down the corridor away from Joe's door. I stopped at the rune line. "It's a long story."

He gave a short laugh. "I've got nothing but time."

Something was different from this morning. He seemed stronger somehow, more life in him. Whatever had been draining his magic was well and truly gone now. The observation almost pleased me, until I remembered the exact opposite was true for Sammy.

"It's my fault," I whispered. "I didn't mean to, but I hurt her."

Arthur's face went serious. He touched my arm, gently. I flinched, but nothing happened. Whatever had infected my skin earlier didn't seem to affect him.

"Tell me what happened," he said.

"Joe and Chloe were playing this game – they made these vines grow and they lifted me up in the air." My stomach lurched at the memory of the sensation. It had been almost fun at the time, but now it made me want to throw up. "Then

Chloe got pissed off, and... I don't know. The vines started strangling me."

"She tried to hurt you?"

I shook my head. "No, I don't think so... I don't know."

"But she hurt Sammy?"

"No." That part I was sure of. "*I* hurt Sammy. After the vines dropped away, my magic started floating away from me. It left these dark patches on my skin, and Sammy touched one of them." I risked a glance at my arm. The ashy spots were still there, singed into my limbs. I shuddered and looked away.

Arthur shook his head. "That doesn't... Your magic can't just float away, can it?"

I shrugged. That wasn't the important part. "I don't know. But it was the same as with you and Miss Caraway. I could feel this icy rush of air, but this time it was coming from inside me. I couldn't stop it."

Arthur stared at me. He clearly didn't understand anything I was saying, but then a flash of recognition crossed his face. "I remember that feeling," he said quietly. He touched his stomach. "But it wasn't air."

"It was filled with ash," I said. "I could taste it on the vines, and—"

"No, Ursula, it wasn't air. It was magic. I remember now. It was draining my magic."

"What was?" I desperately hoped he wouldn't say Chloe, but deep down, I knew it had to be her. I'd seen the flash of light just before everything went wrong. It must have been a rune. She'd been trying to control me, trying to steal my magic, and Sammy had got caught in the middle of it.

"I..." Arthur hesitated; his eyes flicked back and forth as if the memory was just out of reach. "I don't know how to explain it," he said finally. "But it was someone else's magic draining mine. I could feel it."

"They should have let me help Sammy. I think I'm the only one who can." I'd never said anything so arrogant in my whole life, but suddenly, I was absolutely sure it was true. If my parents didn't let me try to stop the magic draining Sammy, then there was no chance anyone else could.

Arthur studied my face. "You really think you can help her?"

"I'm sure of it. But there's no way they'll let me. I'd have to get to her before anyone notices, but there's no way I can reach the sick bay before Ben and Chloe do."

"I think I can help with that."

"Yeah?"

He nodded. "Do you trust me?"

"I..."

He grabbed my hand, not waiting for an answer.

"What are you—?" I didn't get a chance to finish the question. Arthur closed his eyes, and it was like the lights had gone out with it. Darkness slammed down on us, knocking the air from my chest. I tried to breathe in, but my chest shuddered instead. It wasn't darkness; it was nothingness. We were in a vacuum, and I was going to suffocate.

The lights came back on, slamming into me just like the darkness had. I gasped, an awful wheezing sound coming out of my chest. Arthur wrapped his arms around me before I collapsed.

"I know," he said. "It's awful the first time. It gets better."

I nodded, though I couldn't imagine ever letting him do that again. He lowered me to the floor, and I sat, sucking air back into my lungs.

Voices came from the next room – my mother's and Miss Caraway's, and maybe the entire staff who weren't zombies. I couldn't make out the words, but their voices rose and fell in sharp peaks, anger and worry tumbling out as they argued about how to help Sammy. I pressed a finger to my lips, shushing Arthur, though I was the one making all the noise.

We were in a bedroom – or at least a space for students to convalesce. I could see my mother's touch in here. The bedspread was green, a print of cool, tropical leaves covering it, matching the soothing pale green walls. There were real plants in here, too, but like all of my mother's attempts, they were wilting, soon to succumb to plant death.

Arthur's hand found mine, and he pulled me up. "Come on. We can get to Sammy and heal her before they even decide who they're mad at."

I nodded, though my heart thumped in my ears. With every beat it seemed to say: *"My fault. My fault."*

We crept down the corridor, and Arthur pushed open a door at the far end. "She's in there," he whispered. He stepped back as if to let me go in alone, but I tightened my grip on his hand.

"Come with me," I whispered.

He hesitated, but I could feel it. He *had* to come with me. He had to help me.

"Okay," he said, glancing back down the corridor. "But quickly."

We slipped into the room. Sammy lay on a bed, covered with an identical green-leaf bedspread. More ailing plants surrounded her, along with quickly sketched symbols on the walls, floor and headboard. They created a rough rune line around her, but it wouldn't be enough – she needed much stronger protection magic.

I felt it as I got closer, the rush of icy air running through Sammy.

"I don't understand." I touched my stomach, but the magic no longer ran through me. It veered around, as if afraid to touch me. I tasted ash in my mouth, though, and felt the sandpapery burn of grit and dirt flying past me.

"You say it's all magic?" I asked.

Arthur nodded. "Her magic, being stripped away, just like mine was."

And mine, floating away in sparks. "It really wasn't me," I said, half to myself.

"Of course not." Arthur shook his head. "I don't know what you saw, but you didn't cause this."

"Except, I did. Or, not me, but..." Someone had used me. *Chloe* had used me, controlling me with that sparking rune.

She hadn't taken much of *my* magic, but she'd sent that rush of air running through me, those sparks flying out from me, in order to steal Sammy's. Did it latch on to her just because she had touched me? Or had my magic targeted her because she was my geminus pair?

Sammy groaned, and we both turned back towards the bed. She didn't stop, the sound turning into a long moan. Arthur shook his head. "That didn't... that's not from the magic."

"No?"

Sammy's whole body seemed to contract, curling her forward. My heart plummeted. "She's going to have the baby... but it's too early, isn't it?"

"Can you still help her?" Arthur asked.

I nodded. "Yes," I said, my voice coming out more confident than I really felt. I could make sure her baby survived; I would have to. Sammy had said she wasn't sure if her baby would have magic, but suddenly I could feel her – the tiny child and her power surging around her.

"We have to wrap her in protection," I told Arthur. "Both of them – her and the baby."

He nodded, though I could tell he didn't understand what I meant. Sammy moaned again, her unconscious state not deep enough to protect her from the pain. I took hold of one of her hands, clutching tight to Arthur's with the other. He did the same, taking Sammy's free hand and closing the link between the three of us. I took a thread of magic, visualising it as bright red in my mind, and drew a line from the top of Sammy's head. I traced all the way around her shoulders, down her arm and over the outline of each of her fingers. Arthur followed me, winding his magic over mine, until the two threads merged together into a hard, protective barrier.

Sammy's eyes opened, a scream escaping her lips. I gripped her hand as tight as I could. "Keep going," I hissed at Arthur.

Sammy's body contorted, pulling away from us, but I couldn't break the thread. We traced down her side, around one leg and then the other, and then back up to her other arm.

Sweat beaded on my forehead, and my palms felt slick against Sammy's and Arthur's. Sammy's scream petered out, and a third strand of magic appeared – Sammy's, stretching out to join ours. She didn't speak, the strains on her body and mind too great, but her eyes met mine, and there was life in them again.

A small part of my mind was conscious that the raised voices from the other room had dropped to a normal volume, that they had finished arguing, and were instead working together to come up with a plan. Soon, they would walk down the corridor to implement whatever they had come up with. A bigger part of my mind was focused on the heaviness creeping up my body like a black sticky tar.

"You can do this, Ursula," Arthur dug his nails into my palm, and the pain woke me a little. "I know you're tired but keep going!"

Sammy's hand tightened on mine too. I nodded, my head lolling with the movement. Keep going... I could do that. Sammy was about to give birth, and yet they were encouraging *me*.

It struck me as unfair that Arthur was still so alert, even after being so sick. Why could he manage to do magic without it exhausting him the way it did me? Perhaps he had had more practice, or perhaps he was like Ben and Chloe, pulling energy from everything around them. No wonder Mum's plants always died. No wonder the workers all looked like zombies.

My eyes snapped open. "They look like zombies," I repeated aloud.

Chloe had never been able to beat Ben, but suddenly her magic was so much stronger. It wasn't the geminus connection increasing her power, and my dad wasn't controlling the workers. It was all her.

And that's how we could stop her – cut her power off at the source. We had to get everyone out.

I turned to Arthur to tell him, but the heavy tar creeping up my body had reached my head. "They have to go," was all I managed, and then I felt Arthur catch me, as the tar took me over.

Chapter Eight

Time blurred. I felt myself moving, but it was as if I was being carried. Then I was lying in a bed, everything hazy. I woke at one point and my sister was holding my hand.

"Fight back, little mouse," she whispered.

Magic pulled at me, or rather, something pulled my magic away. It stretched out from me like shining cobwebs, sparking every so often as pieces broke off.

I gathered them back to me, reaching out with both my mind and my arms to clutch at handfuls. I caught hold of them, but something felt wrong. The magic wasn't all mine.

My sister squeezed my hand, and energy seeped off her. Threads of her magic wrapped around me, burrowing their way into my skin. I tried to pull away, but she squeezed tighter, tugging at me. I looked up, and her eyes were wide, but blank, glowing almost. I didn't recognise anything behind them.

I JOLTED AWAKE. THE sick bay room was light, the curtains half closed, and a bright column of evening sunlight streamed through the gap. I was alone, the chair where my sister had sat now empty.

I scrambled out of the bed. I had to stop her.

My muscles ached as if I had been running, and the hair at the back of my neck stuck to my skin in damp, sweaty mats. The green, leafy bedspread lay bunched at my feet, like I'd spent the night thrashing, fighting against whatever Chloe had tried to do to me.

No more. I forced my feet into steps, into a run.

I raced down the hallway, trailing along the twists and turns of corridors. An eerie quiet greeted me at every step. Runes ran across the floor, line after line of them. That's where the silence came from. The symbols had thrown the building into a stasis. They kept everything in place, stopped the magic from moving between rooms. Even I could barely cross them, my whole body buzzing every time I stepped over one.

Finally, I found some of the workers. None of them spoke to me – none even made eye contact. They all sat or stood in a stretch of corridor, staring hauntingly into nothing. They weren't just zombies. Bones jutted out under their skin, muscles withering away along with their energy, and burnt patches marked their limbs. They'd been drained of everything but the reflex to inhale and exhale.

I approached one of them. He sat in a chair, and our faces were almost level, yet his eyes still didn't meet mine. "Run," I said. "Get out of here."

He didn't even sway.

"Go!" I yelled. "All of you, leave. Now!"

Still nothing. I grabbed his arm, pouring power into the gesture. The man finally stood, not running, but slowly shambling forward. He stopped as soon as he got to a rune line, his whole body seeming to shut down.

I shoved him, forcing him over the line. "Keep going," I told him. "All of you, keep going."

But he only took a few more steps. Anger coiled in my stomach. "Go!" I screamed. "Go, you useless zombies!" I shoved him again, harder and harder. "Go!"

Power erupted from me.

He stumbled forward, gasping. "What the…?" He turned towards me, his eyes clearing but horror building in them. Magic flared on my skin, propelling the worker away.

He was right to be horrified. All the magic I'd ever kept hidden was rising to the surface. Around us, the other workers woke from their daze.

"Run," I said, my voice low and resonant. "Go now!"

They scrambled over each other in their escape, nothing uniform in their movements now. I let myself breathe as they did, but my power didn't retreat back inside me. It stayed humming on my skin. My whole body changed with it, my spine straightening and chest opening out. I felt elated… I felt powerful… But behind that was something darker I couldn't quite identify. I had cut off Chloe's source of energy by freeing the workers, yet a sense of impending danger still ran through the walls of the school. I felt the magic bubbling up, ready to swallow all of us.

I turned, running in the opposite direction to the workers, towards my sister. All around the school, I felt other workers leaving, the very building seeming to shift with their exit. A pungent smell of rotting plants came from the main foyer, but so did light. I ran towards it, eager for any signs of life.

"It's out of control!"

I slowed as I heard my father's voice. He sounded agitated, and I remembered the rise and fall of words as my parents had argued about how to help Sammy.

Sammy. Where was she? *How* was she?

Heavy footsteps strode across the foyer towards me, and I shrank back against the wall, slipping behind a wilted Ficus plant.

"We're going to have to strip her of her powers," my father said.

My stomach clenched. I stepped back automatically, clutching my newly unlocked magic to me. It spilled out around me, no forcing it back inside now.

Stripping away my magic would be like carving away pieces of my skin. How could they do that to Chloe? It didn't matter what she'd done, that was too cruel a punishment. Something niggled at the back of my mind, and I shook my head, trying to force the memories to solidify.

"Fight back, little mouse."

Why had Chloe said that if she was the one causing all of this?

"Surely that has to be a last resort," my mother said. "What about the boy?"

The boy... did she mean Joe? Would the geminus bond mean his powers would be stripped too?

"I'm afraid we're already at the last resort stage."

I peeked out from behind the Ficus. Miss Caraway stood with my parents, still in that ridiculous floral dress. She wore a coat over it, and a duffle bag lay at her feet. Was she leaving? I wasn't sure if that made me feel relieved or more frightened.

"The boy is an unfortunate casualty," she said, "but we don't have a choice."

"She's right, Candace. And if it doesn't work, then..." Dad trailed off.

I swallowed. Whatever he was going to say, it couldn't be worse than what I was imagining. My mother looked from Dad to Miss Caraway.

Mum looked even smaller than she had a few days ago. She made a sound that was almost a sob. "This could kill them both."

I gasped, slapping a hand over my mouth. Mum looked up, alarm firing in her eyes, and Dad turned slowly towards me. "Chloe?" he called. His voice boomed with a power that didn't quite reach me. I turned and fled.

"Ursula..."

I heard Mum race after me, but I didn't look back.

"Ursula, wait!" she called again, but her footsteps came to a halt, like always. She had never fought for us. She had always just given up.

My own feet thudded against the stairs, making a dull, echoing sound in the silence. I didn't stop running until I reached our floor, even though no one was chasing me. What did it mean that they hadn't – why wouldn't they follow? Were they that afraid of Chloe? Had her power become so strong that even my parents cowered away, hiding behind rune lines?

I passed my sister's room, glancing in. She wasn't in there, her empty bed unmade. The mouse cage sat in the middle of it, open and abandoned, no sign of the rodents she had been try-ing to control.

I reached Ben's room and threw open the door. "Ben…" I couldn't get anything else out. I leaned forward, out of breath.

He looked up at me, startled. "Little mouse… you're awake." His voice didn't hold the same laughter it usually did when he used my nickname. His eyebrows drew together in a frown. He stood, moving towards me, and placing his hand gently on my shoulder.

I panted, still trying to get my breath back. "It's Chloe," I choked out.

Ben sat down on the bed, drawing me to sit next to him. "What's she done now?"

"They're going to strip her powers." I shivered, all the heat from running rushing out of me. "She's the one behind it. She's been stealing energy."

Ben's frown deepened. "What do you mean?"

I shook my head. "Can't you feel it? She's draining the whole building. It's like you do with the plants, but bigger. The workers look dead on their feet. But it's okay, I sent them away. She won't be able to steal their power anymore."

"You did what?" His voice had an edge to it, and his hand suddenly felt heavy on my shoulder.

"I sent the workers away – cut her off at the source. But you're missing the point. I heard Mum and Dad talking about stripping Chloe's magic. They said they have no other options."

Ben's grip on me tightened. "They can't do that!" His fingers bit into my skin and I squirmed away. He released me but didn't apologise. He stood, moving away from the bed.

"I know," I said. "It could kill her, and Joe too! I know she's done some bad things, but—"

"It doesn't matter what she's done!" Ben spun around as if he would strike me.

I shrank back against the bed. "That's what I'm saying," I said quietly. He didn't seem to hear me.

"I have to find her." His hand massaged his bottom lip, hard enough to tear it

Something in my stomach unclenched when he said that. I wanted to help my sister... or maybe I didn't, maybe I just wanted to stop her. Either way, I didn't know what to do. I wanted Ben to do it. I wanted him to take over.

A noise outside the room caught my attention. Ben's head whipped up, staring out into the corridor. "Chloe...?"

Footsteps thudded against the floorboards, just as mine had done only moments before. Ben hesitated for only a second, and then he was off down the corridor, chasing after her.

I stood, taking a few steps after them. "Wait," I yelled. But they were both gone.

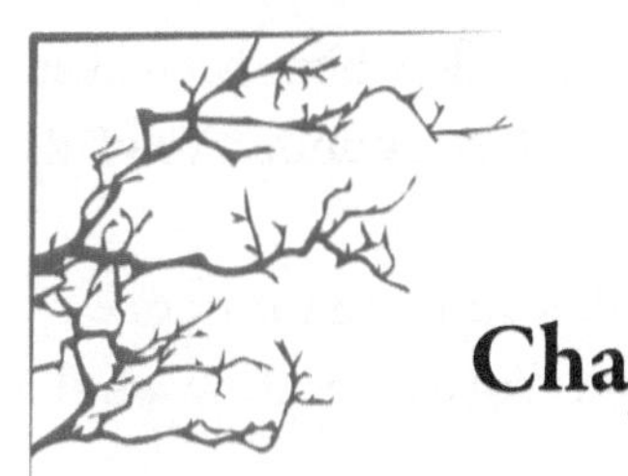

Chapter Nine

I sat on the bed for a long time, waiting for them to come back. The unnatural silence of the building settled over me, and I shivered. Eventually, I couldn't stand it any longer, and I made my way back to my own room.

Warm cosiness greeted me. I reached out, and echoes of my own magic reached back, welcoming me home. A humming came from the floor. No, not from the floor – from Arthur's room below mine. He was in there, his magic stretching out to meet mine.

I'm coming, I whispered back to it.

My mother had placed some kind of ward on the door to the dormitory floor. I felt it trying to push against me, to turn me away. If my magic had been weaker – if I hadn't unlocked all of it just an hour earlier – it would have worked.

More rune lines crossed the floor inside – layers and layers of them, drawn over multiple times. Voices came from Arthur's room, but I didn't immediately turn that way. Fingers of ash spread out from the library, almost as if they were reaching for the runes. The lines bent around them, the symbols curving to fit. Had they been drawn that way or had the runes moved to avoid the ash? I stepped towards them, reaching out to feel the hum of both sets of magic competing against each other.

"We have to get out of here," Joe hissed.

I froze. I stepped backwards and the floorboards creaked under my foot. Silence stretched, then feet pounded towards Arthur's door.

"Get the hell away from us!" Joe flew through the doorway, his hand raised in front of him, fingers splayed as if he would hurl magic at me.

I took another step back, raising my own hands in defence. Arthur appeared beside Joe, grabbing his arm. "It's Ursula. It's just Ursula."

Joe dropped his hands, relief and horror crossing his face. Arthur stepped towards me, pulling me into a hug. "You're awake."

I sank into the embrace, relief filling me. He pulled back to look at me. "And your magic is different."

I dropped my gaze, ashamed to admit how much I had been hiding until now. "Is Sammy okay?" I asked.

Arthur squeezed my arms gently, then released me. "Yeah, she's in here."

Joe stood back to let us into the room, and Arthur drew me inside, shutting the door behind us. Sammy sat propped up in the bed, the tiniest baby I'd ever seen on her chest. A weight lifted inside me at seeing them both healthy.

Joe's face softened as he looked at them. "Ursula, meet Calliope – Callie."

Sammy held out her hand, beckoning me over. "She's here because of you. You saved us."

I moved forward but didn't dare touch the child. "She's beautiful."

Magic swirled around her – Sammy's, Joe's, Arthur's, mine and her own. The protection around her was strong; Chloe wouldn't be able to touch her. But still, she was so tiny. This wasn't a safe place for her.

I looked around at my classmates. Dark shadows marked their eyes, and heavy weariness shrouded all of them. "You're trying to leave," I said.

Sammy hesitated and her eyes darted away from mine as if she was afraid of my reaction.

I frowned. "I think it's a good idea."

Sammy and Joe looked at each other, then he moved closer to the bed and put his arm around her. There was a greyish tinge to his skin that wasn't there before. "We want out," he told me. "We all do. The magic is getting to us."

Something didn't seem right about Joe's words. The way he said *we*. If they were all in agreement, why didn't they just go? And why had they been afraid to tell me? Suddenly, it dawned on me. The ward on the door... the rune lines... My parents had trapped them in here.

I had got those workers across the lines, but it would be different with my classmates. I could already feel there was strong magic around them, keeping them here. Magic I wasn't sure I knew how to break.

I didn't know if I could help them – I didn't know if I could get them out – but I owed them the truth. It was the least I could do after the destruction my family had caused.

"I got the builders out," I told them, "but I don't know if I can do the same for you. I promise I will try."

I saw it register on Joe and Sammy's faces then – they could see the change in my magic, just as Arthur had. Joe shifted, perhaps uncomfortable with my strength.

"I can't come with you," I said, ignoring his unease. "My parents want to strip Chloe's magic, but it might hurt Joe too. It could even kill both of you."

My words seemed to hit Sammy like a physical blow. "No..." she whispered. She shook her head, fiercely. "That can't... they can't do that!"

Joe's arm tightened around her shoulder. "Shouldn't I have been able to tell if Chloe's causing this?" he asked. "Our magic is supposed to be twinned."

And she's my sister, I nearly said. Instead, I shook my head. "I think she's got really good at hiding things."

Should *I* have known? Should I have been able to tell what she was up to? But I'd never known what Chloe was doing, even before the geminus magic.

Maybe that was the problem.

Joe and Sammy looked at each other, then down at Calliope, another silent conversation happening between them. Joe squeezed Sammy's hand, and she nodded.

"We're staying," she said. "We can't let them strip Chloe's power. Not if it could hurt her and Joe."

Joe nodded. "Use your magic to fix this; don't waste it on getting us out."

Arthur moved closer to me, offering me his strength too. They all stared at me, determination and belief in their eyes. I felt their trust in me – their faith in my newly unlocked magic. There was just one problem with that. I had no clue how to fix this.

When had it all gone so wrong? Had Chloe always been dangerous, and I just hadn't seen it? Had the geminus magic damaged her in some way, warping her powers? No. It had started before that, I was sure of it. It had started…

Suddenly, it hit me. I opened the door and strode back out into the corridor.

Arthur followed after me. "Where are you going? This is the only safe place."

"Nowhere is safe until we fix this."

A flash of Chloe sitting beside the bed holding my hand came into my mind. *Fight back, little mouse.* There was more to this, I was sure of it.

I walked towards the library door. Joe and Arthur followed me, and then a moment later Sammy did too, clutching Callie to her chest with one hand and leaning heavily against the wall with the other.

I sent a wave of healing magic out to her, trying to ease some of her pain. I felt Joe do the same, and Sammy stood up straighter, her body responding and gaining strength.

"You should stay in bed," I told her. She shook her head, though she tightened her grip on Callie.

I traced the lines of ash with my eyes. This was where it had started, where Chloe and Ben first lost control of their magic, where Mum and Dad first realised we were all part of geminus pairs. Would I have eventually lost control if Sammy and I hadn't found each other? But then why hadn't Chloe and Joe's magic stabilised now they were together?

I turned to Joe. "What did you mean when you said the magic started to get to you?

His hand went to his wrist, one of Sammy's silver bracelets circling it. "I don't know. It's like Miss Caraway said about the geminus magic – that it can become dangerous. I could feel it exploding inside me, making me change. I couldn't control it."

"But the geminus pair is supposed to stop that."

Joe shook his head. "I think maybe Miss Caraway got it wrong. My magic only gets calmer when I'm around you three. It's way worse around Chloe and Ben."

That seemed to fit with what I was thinking. Chloe wasn't in control of her magic anymore, so how could she possibly help calm someone else's? There was only one thing for it. I took another step towards the library.

"Where are you going?" Sammy called after me.

I didn't answer. Numb emptiness hit me as I crossed the rune line, the magical vacuum pulling me forward. Sammy gasped, and Joe swore. They felt it too, even without crossing the line.

"What is that?" Arthur asked.

"Ursula, come back. Don't go down there!" Sammy's voice held a note of panic, but I kept walking.

"This is where it started. Where Chloe first lost control of her magic." I opened the door.

Books lay strewn across the floor, and a dull, muffled blanket of dust, ash and silence fell over me. Suddenly, I understood why it felt like a vacuum. Chloe had sucked every ounce of energy out of the books – out of the room itself. No wonder she had started a fire. She had overloaded herself.

Arthur and Joe crept into the room after me, peering around at the destruction. Sammy stayed in the doorway; her hands clasped protectively over Callie.

"Who's been in here?" I turned back to the others.

Arthur shook his head. "None of us. I didn't know there was anything down here."

I looked to Sammy and Joe, and they shook their heads too.

"No, the closest I got was when I asked you about the rune line," Sammy said.

"Honestly, I forgot about it after that.

So had I – almost. That must have been part of my mother's spell. I picked up a book that was lying open, face down. The pages were coated in grime. I brushed them off, revealing a spell on removing excess magic. Arthur took it from me, examining the page.

I picked up another book, and this time it fell open on a page about severing magical connections. The spells in these pages reminded me of something, but it wouldn't quite come clear. I'd read something in the encyclopaedia of spells, and it floated just at the edge of my memory, almost as if it was trying to signal its own importance.

Joe picked up a third book from the floor. "Symptoms and side effects of stolen magic," he read.

"She's trying to fix it," I said. "She knows she's losing control."

"She already *has* lost control!" Arthur took the book from me, skimming through the pages.

The others all looked alarmed by the discovery, but I felt a lightness inside my chest for the first time in days. Chloe was trying to fix it. My sister was still in there, trying to regain control of the magic.

Fight back, little mouse.

My eyes fell on Sammy. She still stood by the door, rocking slightly as she soothed Callie. Her eyes traced around the room, almost as if she were looking for something in particular.

"You wrote something about this, didn't you?" I said.

Her gaze shot to mine, eyes almost guilty. She hesitated, then nodded. "I've written a lot, but most of it's still jumbled. I can only read a few pages."

I touched the bracelets on my wrist. "But it told you we needed to enchant these?"

"Yeah, my writings told me we would do it. I don't know why; they don't seem to help."

I ran a finger over the silver bands, letting them clink together. "I do," I said. The plan was only just starting to form in my mind, but I said it with as much confidence as I could muster. I needed them to follow me. I needed them to trust me, and I needed to trust myself.

"I read something in one of the textbooks about using objects to control magic." I slipped one of the bracelets from my wrist, squeezing it tightly, letting the metal cut into my palm. I'd never got further than F in the encyclopaedia, but that didn't matter. B for bracelet – B for binding spell.

"We're going to use these to bind Chloe."

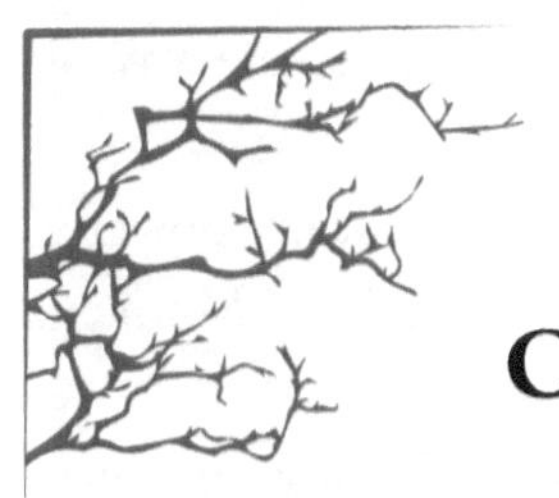

Chapter Ten

I found Ben downstairs, no sign of Chloe. When I saw him, I almost backed away. He sat on the bottom step, his head in his hands, and everything about him screamed broken.

I could tell from the way he stiffened that he'd heard me approach, but he didn't turn around. I sat down next to him, bumping my shoulder against his.

"Did you find Chloe?" I asked. It was a silly question – he wouldn't be sitting there if he had.

Ben shook his head. "No."

He rubbed at his face. His skin had turned red, where he'd been worrying at his temple. Obviously, my parents hadn't found Chloe either. She and Joe were safe for a little longer at least.

"We went into the library," I told him.

His head shot up. "I told you not to."

"I know, but she's been in there. We found these books, and..." I didn't know how to explain everything we'd found. "It's worse than we thought. I think Chloe's in over her head."

That was the best way to describe it, I decided. I didn't believe that Chloe had done any of this on purpose, and the fact that she was looking up side effects of siphoning magic made me sure she knew what she'd done was bad. I remembered the way her eyes had glowed when she sat by my bedside – so blank and unfamiliar – the way she'd told me to fight it. She was say-ing it to herself too.

"I think that Mum and Dad were right about her power."

Ben pulled away from me. "You can't be serious! Mum and Dad can't take her magic away."

I wasn't even sure they would be able to. The way the magic was behaving – that icy rush of air I'd felt when it was running through me – there was no way to stop once it started. As much as I had tried to dam it up, I couldn't. Geminus magic was even more powerful than they had warned us. If Chloe was stuck in the middle of that, she'd have no way to stop it.

"I know, I know," I said, trying to soothe Ben's ire. "That's not what I meant." I chewed on my lip. I should have got Joe or Sammy to come with me. Ben still saw me as a baby – his little mouse of a sister. But I wasn't so small anymore. I could fix this, if only he would listen to me.

"I want to bind her instead," I told him. "I read about it in one of those textbooks from the classroom."

Ben's forehead creased with a frown. "Bind her?"

I nodded. "It won't take her magic away permanently; it will just stop her using it. It will still all be inside her."

Ben started to shake his head, then hesitated. He rubbed his fingers together as if reassuring himself his own power was all still there. "Her magic will all be intact? You're sure?"

"As sure as I can be." The textbooks hadn't gone into specifics about what happened after the binding, but it couldn't be worse than her and Joe dying, could it?

Ben nodded slowly. "That sounds... well, it doesn't sound awful," he said, finally.

"Not awful" was probably about as good as we could hope for right now. I just prayed my parents would see it that way.

Ben stood and reached out a hand. I let him pull me up. "We have to find Chloe first," I told him.

He made a noise in his throat. "No, let's go back to the library. I think I can draw her there."

My stomach flipped a little at the idea of going back to that burnt-out room. Honestly, it creeped me out. Mum had been right to block it off with runes. "Why there?"

Ben grimaced. "It's where this all started," he said, his voice heavy. I could hear the regret in his tone. It wasn't just Chloe who had lost control of the magic that day. "It should be where we end it." He turned, walking away before I had a chance to ask anything else.

SAMMY STAYED IN THE doorway, not coming all the way into the library. She'd put Callie down for a nap in Arthur's room, and she hovered between the two rooms. We'd wrapped the room in protective magic, but her eyes still darted towards the crib at every hint of noise.

"You can stay with her, if you want," I told her. "You don't have to be a part of this."

She smiled, but there was something sad in her eyes. "I think I do."

I frowned. She'd read something. She might not know exactly what was going to happen, but it was obvious she had an idea of how things were going to play out.

Sammy shook herself off, smiling lightly. "Besides, Callie's safe in there," she said. "I trust your magic."

I touched the bracelets. "*Our* magic. Let's hope this works."

She nodded, then hesitated. She drew her notebook out of her pocket. "I think you should have this. I finished the last page last night."

I frowned. "But I can't read it."

"You will be able to, when the time's right."

That sounded like the kind of thing my mum said when I got frustrated about home schooling and all the other things we weren't allowed to do. I clutched the book to my chest, then slipped it under my shirt to keep it safe. "Thank you."

"All right." Ben clapped his hands, drawing our attention to him. "I want you to gather piles of ash. Bring them all into the centre of the room."

I glanced down at the debris beneath our feet. Images of those long, dark, shadowy fingers reaching for me played in my mind, and I shuddered. The ash was magically charged, I could feel that even from here, and I didn't want to touch it.

"It will help," Ben said. "I'm going to draw Chloe here, and I need to use material from a spell she cast. Bring all of it in – right from the corners of the room."

Ben headed towards one corner of the room, and Joe to another, so I took the third. Arthur followed me, dropping into a crouch beside me as I swept ash into my hands.

"Are you sure about this?" he whispered.

I looked up at him, frowning. "I thought you were on board with binding Chloe."

"I am. It's just..." Arthur hesitated, and his eyes flicked towards Ben. Ben's back was to us, and Arthur took my hand, pulling me out into the corridor. "I didn't realise you were going to involve your brother," he said.

"Why wouldn't I?"

Arthur chewed on his lip, staring back into the room. "The way he uses magic worries me sometimes."

Sammy was back in Arthur's room, singing to Callie. The lullaby made a strangely ominous soundtrack to Arthur's words. I'd never seen Ben use magic in bad ways – that had always been Chloe's department.

"What do you mean?"

Arthur made a noise in his throat. "That night in town when we went out and he started throwing fireworks at people..."

"Wait, *Ben* was throwing fireworks?"

Arthur had told me and Sammy about the fireworks when we were up on the barn roof, but I'd thought he meant Chloe. Had he actually ever said that, or had I just jumped to conclusions, blaming my sister as I always did? To be fair, if there was a chaotic spell happening, she was usually the one behind it.

"Yeah..." Arthur shook his head, as if brushing off images. "He just seems really different when he uses magic. It's like it takes him over."

I frowned trying to fit that image of my brother to the one I knew and loved. The only times I'd really seen him work strong magic were when he fought Chloe. But that was different – Dad made him do that.

"I don't know..." I said finally. "Maybe he was just drunk that night. Alcohol makes people do strange things, right?"

"Sometimes, I guess." Arthur didn't sound sure.

"Ursula, what are you doing?" Ben called. "Come help us."

I glanced at Arthur. He shrugged, but didn't turn away. "Up to you," he said. "If you're sure it's okay."

I hesitated. Ben was my safe sibling – he always had been. This had to be okay. "I'm sure," I told Arthur.

Ben had arranged piles of ash in the middle of the room. He beckoned for us to come closer. "All of you, stand near this one. It represents us."

Joe, Arthur and I dutifully moved to stand beside the pile of ash as directed. Sammy stayed out in the corridor, looking in from the doorway. I knew there was no such thing as good and black magic, only the intentions of the person using it. Even so, involving the remains of a fire like this felt dark. Arthur's hand slipped into mine, and I squeezed his.

Ben drew out a long thread of magic, then started to draw runes around the second pile of ash.

"What is he doing?" Joe asked.

I watched the magic, transfixed. "It looks like that leading spell," I said.

"What leading spell?"

I dragged my eyes away from Ben, turning to face Joe. "The one you taught Chloe – the one she was practising on the mice."

He frowned. "What mice?"

"The ones you bought at the pet store. You know... she used the same spell on the vines too, to make them grow upwards."

Joe shook his head slowly. "I didn't teach her that. I'd never seen it before."

I frowned. Why would Chloe have lied about that? "Then where did she learn it?"

He shrugged. "Looks like your brother's the expert."

I turned back towards Ben. The pile of ash representing Chloe was shifting, slowly inching towards the one at our feet, drawn along by the thread.

What was it Chloe had said to Ben after the vines? *I wouldn't have had to if you hadn't...* She never finished the sentence.

I watched Ben now, his loop of magic drawing the pile of ash closer. My stomach dropped. Surely, this could only work if he had already looped a thread of magic around her, giving him control.

"Oh no." I let go of Arthur's hand, jerking forward. Sammy's notebook fell from under my shirt as I did. "Ben stop, please!"

He raised a hand, holding me off, and like the silly little mouse I was, I froze.

Joe picked up the notebook. "This is Sammy's. Why do you have it? Did she give it to you?" He opened the book, and a note fell out, written in Sammy's spidery writing.

I stared at the page it had marked, horror setting in as a string of words became clear.

Their magic will flare out of control, and she will realise she is under her brother's power...

That's what Chloe had read that day in the classroom. If Ben made those fireworks that night in town, then he was the one who had got the ash on Arthur's cheek. He was the one who had marked him with the magic that made him sick. And everything that Chloe had done had been because Ben was influencing her.

Joe picked up the note that had dropped from the book. "What the hell?" He looked up at me, his eyes wide. He held the page out to me.

Take my daughter to my mother, it read. *Keep Calliope safe.*

I spun around, searching for Sammy's figure outside the doorway. Sammy thought something was going to happen to her. She *knew* something was going to happen to her. Joe met my eye, the same realisation clear in his expression. He turned to run, but the ash swirled up in front of us, pushing him back. It drew itself into lines, forming runes in the air.

"Ursula, what is this?" Arthur clutched my arm.

I slashed a hand through the air, scattering the runes. "Ben, stop!"

But it was too late. Chloe walked into the room, drawn by Ben's magic.

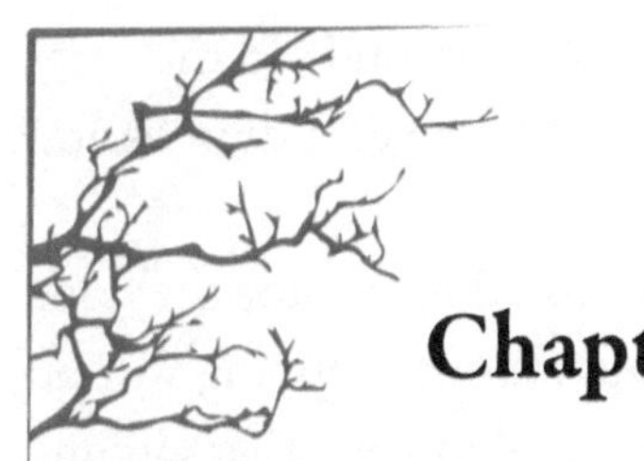

Chapter Eleven

I'd been so stupid. *Ben* was the one who drew magic from the plants, killing them each time. Ben was the one desperate to increase his powers. Why had I been so quick to blame my sister? I knew the answer, though I didn't want to admit it. Because Chloe was Chloe – complicated and prickly.

But Ben was the one who had always been stronger, and he was the one who always won.

Chloe strained against the magic now, fighting with every step. "Don't do this, Ben, please!" she whispered. "You have to stop."

Fight back, little mouse... She'd been saying it to herself as much as me.

I turned to Joe and Arthur. "We've made a mistake." My voice came out as a whisper too. "It's Ben – he's the one controlling this."

Joe's eyes were wild. "I have to help Sammy!"

"Go!" I told him. Did Sammy really believe she wouldn't survive this? That couldn't be true. We *all* had to get through this, somehow.

Joe hesitated. He looked between me and Arthur. "If anything bad happens to me and Sammy, you look after Callie, yeah? You make sure she's safe and that she knows I love her."

"Of course. We'll protect her," Arthur said, at the same time as I said, "Nothing bad is going to happen." I didn't know if either answer was true.

Joe gave a firm, single nod. He turned to run for the door, but then froze. His limbs seemed to short out, stopping abruptly in a way that would have been comical in any other circumstance. Only his eyes still moved. They roved now, panic lighting behind them.

Sammy gasped from the doorway. "Joe!" She jerked forward as if to step into the room.

"Don't! Don't come in here." Chloe let out a hiccupping sob. "It's the geminus magic."

I saw it then – the cord of shimmering, silvery energy stretching from Chloe to Joe, like the one between me and Sammy. Anything Ben did to Chloe, he would also do to Joe. That was why Joe had felt worse – like the magic was taking him over – when he was around my sister. *Ben's* magic had been taking over Chloe and rippling out to Joe.

I met Chloe's eyes and opened my mouth, but all words froze on my lips. *I wouldn't have had to if you hadn't...* She'd been trying to stop Ben. I'd seen the rune flash in the air just before the vines, and blamed her, but it was Ben all along. Chloe hadn't been trying to hurt me, she'd seen Ben start to drain my magic and was trying to disrupt him.

Sammy looked between Joe and the room where Callie slept, her face stricken. *Stay there*, I said inside my head. We all had to get out of this room, out of this house. As if he'd heard me, Arthur's arm tightened on mine. He took a step towards the door, pulling me with him.

Ben turned towards us, almost like he'd only just remembered we were there. He studied our faces, reading the fear and horror that must have oozed from every inch of us. "Ursula, come here," he said calmly. "Give me the bracelets."

I shook my head. Arthur's grip turned to a stranglehold, his fingers biting into my arm. He took another step towards the door, and I stumbled after him.

Ben frowned. "Don't be silly, little mouse, come here." His voice was so steady – so normal. "I know it's hard, but Chloe's magic is out of control. You know we have to bind her."

I swallowed. "Why are you doing this?"

"Doing what? This was your plan, Urse." Even now, he was still holding on to the lie. He gave me a small, encouraging smile and held out his hand. When I didn't move, his face hardened. "Get over here, Ursula. Mum and Dad will strip her powers otherwise."

"Let them!" Chloe screamed. "It's better than you having them."

"Chloe, no…" I could barely get the words out. "It could kill you and Joe."

She'd tried to make me see what was happening to her by showing me the spell with the mice, and I hadn't understood it. I stared at her, trying to communicate silently how sorry I was, but she wasn't looking at me. Her eyes met Joe's, searching them. He stared back, and then slowly, deliberately, he blinked once.

Chloe nodded back. Just as slowly, just as deliberately. And then she threw back her head. "Mum!" she screamed. "Dad!" She poured power into the word, amplifying it and calling them to us.

"Stop it!" Ben lunged forward, aiming for Chloe. I got in his way, and Arthur ran to protect Joe.

"Mum!" I yelled, pouring all my magic into it too.

"Shut up, Ursula! I'm doing this for you." Ben grabbed my arm, yanking two of the silver bracelets off it. "It won't hurt Chloe, so just calm down. I wouldn't even have to do this if you hadn't sent the workers away."

My stomach dropped. I'd meant to weaken Chloe by getting rid of them, but all I'd done was make him double down on draining Chloe's power. "No! I won't let you." I scratched at his face, trying to grab the bracelets back. Arthur hurled himself forward, knocking Ben to the ground. Chloe gasped, and Joe stumbled forward.

"Run!" I yelled. "Arthur's room. Go!"

Joe grabbed Chloe's hand, and together they bolted for the door. Arthur gave a strangled cry and fell back. Joe and Chloe's steps slowed.

"No, keep going!" I yelled. But their movement dragged, magical threads wrapping tighter around them, slowing them to a crawl.

Ben held Arthur down, marking the lines of a rune on his cheek. Ben stood, brushing ash off his hands. He picked up the silver bracelets he'd taken from me and walked towards Chloe, his steps unhurried. She strained to look back at him, her own steps a painful crawl now. When I suggested binding Chloe, Ben didn't ask if it would hurt her; he'd just asked if her magic would still all be intact. He wanted to keep using it, and I'd made it easier for him.

More threads stretched out from him now, wrapping around Joe and Chloe. "All of you need to calm down," he said. "I'm not going to take more power than you can handle."

Chloe let out a strangled sound that was almost a laugh. "What about Joe and Arthur?" Chloe said. "You took more than *they* could handle."

Ben's jaw clenched. "That was an accident. The geminus connections made me stronger than I realised. I have it under control now."

He didn't, but he couldn't see it. Ben stepped towards Chloe, taking hold of her arm almost gently. "I mean it, Clo. I'm doing this for us. You think Dad will stop at you and me? You really think he won't force Ursula and the others to fight next?"

They both turned to look at me, and the threads of magic turned too, slithering towards me and Arthur.

"I can protect myself," I told him.

Ben shook his head, his focus going back to Chloe. "Not against Dad, little mouse," he said. "I had to get strong enough to stop him."

Maybe that had been true once. Maybe he had started stealing energy to protect us from Dad, but he was the one hurting us now. His eyes went wide, shining like Chloe's had.

I brushed the ash off Arthur's cheek, blurring the rune. He'd turned pale, sweat beading on his forehead. "What do we do?" I said under my breath. Arthur just shook his head. He looked like he was going to pass out.

"Ursula?" My mother appeared in the corridor beside Sammy. "Ben, what's going on?" She moved to come in the room, but Ben held up a hand, stopping her. My father stepped through the doorway beside her, but he too stopped at Ben's raised palm.

"Everything's fine. I have it all under control."

"No, he doesn't!" I yelled. "It's him! He's the one—"

Ben turned towards me, and a wave of magic slammed into me. I fell back, dazed. It tasted sweet, and it hummed against my skin in a way that felt familiar. I stretched out my hands, letting the magic settle against me. It was Sammy's, not his – the magic he'd stolen from her.

"Ben, that is enough!" Dad strode towards my brother. "How dare you hit your sister like—"

Another wave slammed into Dad, sending him flying back into Mum. She fell backwards, and both their heads hit the floor with sickening cracks.

"Mum!" Chloe yelled. I tried to yell too, but all that came out was a rush of air.

Ben dropped his hands. "Oh my god, Mum." He took a shaky step towards her. "I didn't mean to..." He crouched beside her, but Mum and Dad didn't move.

I tried to stand, stumbling under the weight of the magic in the room. I caught sight of Sammy, out in the corridor. She stood still, no longer looking between this room and the other. She mouthed something to me.

"What?" I mouthed back.

She mouthed again, and this time I made out the words. "The book." Her prophecy. I reached under my shirt, but it was gone. I scanned the floor, looking for it. Ash coated everything. I dropped to my hands and knees, scraping it aside. Arthur heaved himself up, joining my search, though he could barely move, and I don't think he knew what he was looking for.

Ben took Mum's face in his hands. "I can fix her," he said. He lurched back towards Chloe, grabbing her right wrist, shoving one of the bracelets on it.

"No!" She let out a sob. Threads of his magic tightened around her, keeping her in place.

"Shh... No, it's all right, Clo, I'm not going to hurt you. Just calm down." Ben's tone was gentle – so calm and rational – so like *him*. He was our brother. How could he be doing this? He put the other bracelet on her left wrist. "I just have to get enough power to help Mum."

"Ben..." I stared at the bracelets, holding my breath. This is what we'd planned – *my* plan. I waited for the bracelets to snap together, binding Chloe in place, protecting us by trapping her magic.

Nothing happened. Chloe looked down at her wrists, still free. It hadn't worked. Ben grabbed Chloe's hands, mashing them together. "Why isn't it binding her?"

"Got it!" Arthur pulled Sammy's notebook from under the ash. I grabbed it, opening it to the end, but the pages moved by themselves, flicking to one in the centre.

"What does it say?" Arthur whispered.

I shook my head. "I don't know." I still couldn't read the words. But then, it was like they unfurled in front of me. The letters climbed up my arms and buried themselves into my skin.

"Oh, I get it. Very clever." Ben let out something that was close to a laugh. "I didn't make the bracelets, so I can't control them. Ursula, get over here."

I shrank back, and Arthur moved in front of me, hands raised. He was too weak to work magic, especially with Ben stealing his, but there he was, still trying to protect me. Ben took a step towards us.

"She didn't make them alone." Sammy's voice rang out from the corridor. Ben spun around, and she stared him down, a hardness in her eyes I had never seen.

Ben drew in a long breath. "Fine." He took a step towards Sammy.

She turned and fled.

"Wait!" He ran after her. Joe and Chloe stumbled along behind him, dragged along by the threads of magic.

I leapt up too, scrambling over my unconscious parents. I heard Arthur stumble after me. Sammy's words from the book pounded with each step, like flashes of light in my head. Suddenly, I understood.

I heard a scream. I surged towards it, bursting into the foyer. Ben held Sammy as she struggled against him. Joe and Chloe just stood there, their eyes blank but bright, completely under his power now.

"Bind Chloe now!" he screamed at Sammy.

"I can't!" she gasped. "I told you; I can't do it alone."

Ben rounded on me, his eyes just as blank as Joe and Chloe's. "Come here, Ursula," he growled.

Arthur moved to step in front of me, but I reached for his arm, stopping him. His skin was cold, clammy, and when he turned to look at me, his face was so, so pale.

"Do you have your bracelet on?" I asked.

He nodded, but it was like the movement was too much for him. The last shred of colour drained from his face, and he crumpled, collapsing at my feet. I let go of him, though it felt like a betrayal to do it. "I'm sorry," I whispered. I walked towards my brother, slipping a bracelet from my wrist as I did.

Ben smiled, but there was nothing comforting in it. "Good, little mouse." He said he was trying to help Mum, trying to protect us from Dad, but only hunger for power lit his eyes. He turned towards Chloe. "Bind her," he told me.

Chloe was practically bound already, so tightly wrapped in his magical control. But he wanted more. He always wanted more. I met Sammy's eye, and she gave just the briefest of half nods.

"Okay," I said.

Sammy stomped on his foot, and brought her head back, smashing it into his nose. He let go of her, clutching his face. She ran up the stairs. I grabbed Ben's wrists, shoving the bracelets onto them.

Ben actually had the gall to laugh. "You can't do it alone, little—"

The bracelets snapped together, binding him in place. He looked down at the handcuffs in surprise. "How...?"

"You threw Sammy's magic at me. I had both."

He smiled slowly. "Very clever, little mouse, but do you really believe this will hold me?"

"No." I looked up at Sammy. She grabbed the air in front of her, and the geminus connection sparked. I felt a tug deep inside me, then the wave of energy rippling out. I grabbed Ben and Arthur's connection.

"Now," Sammy screamed.

We both yanked back, snapping the invisible cords of the geminus bonds. Ben and Arthur both howled, a horrifying, animalistic sound. I doubled over, pain setting me on fire. Emptiness rushed in, my connection to Sammy severing.

Alone, you will struggle to control your magic. Miss Caraway's words about geminus magic wielders came back to me suddenly. *In other cases, it becomes dangerous. Explosive even.*

Something was building, rushing up inside me. "Get down!" I yelled.

The wave of power threw us back. It hit the walls, crashing against them. And then everything burst into flames.

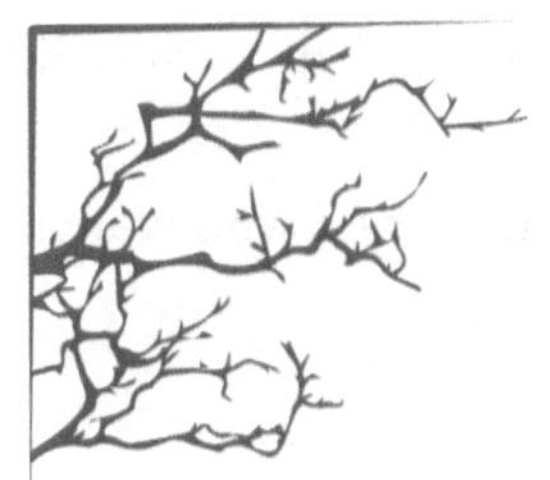

Epilogue

My eyes were open. I blinked to check, but somehow it still felt like I was in a dream. Someone was singing, a quiet lullaby, and cosy warmth surrounded me.

I sat up.

"You're awake." Arthur smiled at me from across the room, then glanced down at the baby in his arms. Callie.

"Oh my god, Callie!" I half rose from the bed, but Arthur raised a hand, gesturing for me to stay.

"It's okay. She's okay. The magic protected her. Miss Caraway and I have been taking turns looking after her."

I sank my head into my hands, relieved. "I didn't know..." I whispered. I hadn't been able to read Sammy's prophecy. I'd only known in the moment what it was asking me to do. I hadn't known that the power would be so strong, or that it would cause an explosion.

Sammy. I felt an ache deep inside me where my connection to her was missing.

"It's okay," Arthur said. "You did what you had to. None of us could have known."

His words didn't make me feel any better. He resumed the lullaby, rocking Callie gently. I watched them, unease building inside me. He'd said he and Miss Caraway had been taking care of Callie.

"Arthur, where's Sammy?" Panic tightened my stomach. "Where's Ben?"

Arthur's eyes slid away from mine. "Everyone who wore a bracelet was protected from the blast."

"But… Oh god, my parents?"

Arthur shook his head slowly. "I'm so sorry."

I pressed a hand to my mouth, not sure if I wanted to throw up or scream. Arthur hesitated, perhaps unsure if he should continue. I couldn't speak, but I gave him a nod. I needed to know.

"The blast severed Ben's connection with the energy in the house – the energy he was draining from the house I mean – but he still had hold of Chloe and Joe. He got free of your binding, and they fled. Miss Caraway had only just got to town. She came back when she sensed the force of the magic."

My siblings were alive. My siblings were alive, but corrupted by selfish, dangerous power. "It was all for nothing," I whispered.

"No!" Arthur shook his head fiercely, waking Callie. She let out a cry, and he rocked her, lowering his voice. "No… not for nothing. Ben would have enslaved or killed us all if you hadn't stopped him. He's considerably less powerful now – considerably less dangerous."

Was that worth my parents' lives? Callie continued to fuss, and he stood, jiggling her gently. He started singing again, his voice strangely haunting.

I watched them, dread growing in my stomach once again. "Arthur, where's Sammy?"

He didn't look up at me, finishing the lullaby. I started to cry, all of it becoming real in one go. "She was at the centre of the blast," he said finally, his voice soft, conscious of the baby in his arms. "I couldn't find..." He swallowed, then moved a hand from around Callie, pulling something from his pocket. A bracelet.

Everyone who wore a bracelet was protected from the blast.

"No..."

"I don't know if it fell off or she took it off, but... I'm so sorry."

The hollow in my stomach where the geminus connection used to be seemed to grow, engulfing me. "She knew it was going to happen." She'd given me the prophecy and that note because she knew she was going to die in trying to stop them. But we didn't stop them. It had all been for nothing.

"She wanted us to take Callie to her mother," I said.

Arthur looked up. "We promised Joe that we'd look after her – that she'd know he loved her."

That was for if he died, but he wasn't dead. What was he now, taken over by magic like my brother and sister? All three of them were trapped in it.

"You can't. You can't tell her anything about him. We have to protect her from them."

"But we promised."

I shook my head. It felt too impossible. The child had to be protected – from her father, from my siblings. Maybe even from us. "So we'll send her letters, or cards or... I don't know. Something."

Arthur swallowed. "There's one more thing."

I closed my eyes. I couldn't take one more thing.

"Sammy's prophecy," he said. "You need to read it."

"I can't. Even before the blast, I couldn't read it. It was like it burrowed into me, telling me what to do."

Arthur was quiet for a moment. "I think you'll be able to read it now."

I opened my eyes and he nodded towards the bedside table, where the battered notebook lay. I opened it, and it flicked automatically to a page. I stared at it, and slowly the gibberish formed into words.

The girl will know only that her mother died, and her grandmother raised her. The magic will be in her, and when the time is right, she will defeat him. She will live sixteen summers before magic finds her, and on her seventeenth birthday, the sky will burst into fire, and it will begin.

I looked at Arthur, not knowing what to say. But he wasn't looking at me. He was staring at Callie. I read the rest of the page, my horror growing with each word.

"It's all going to happen again," I said. "Another three sets of geminus pairs. When Callie is sixteen."

Arthur nodded, still staring down at her. "Yes, and Callie's going to be at the centre of it."

I pressed my hand to my mouth again. "We promised we'd protect her."

"And we will."

"We can't!" The words wrenched themselves out of me, the awfulness of all of it seeming to pour out with them. "I just exploded the school. I destroyed everything!"

Arthur finally looked up at me. "So, we rebuild," he said, simply. "And in sixteen years' time, we'll be ready."

End of Book Three

Enjoyed this book?

You can make a big difference.

REVIEWS ARE THE MOST powerful tool when it comes to getting attention for my books.

As an indie author, it can be hard to get my books into the hands of readers, but honest reviews help me do just that.

If you've enjoyed this book, I would be very grateful if you could spend just a few minutes leaving a review (it can be as short as you like).

Thank you very much!

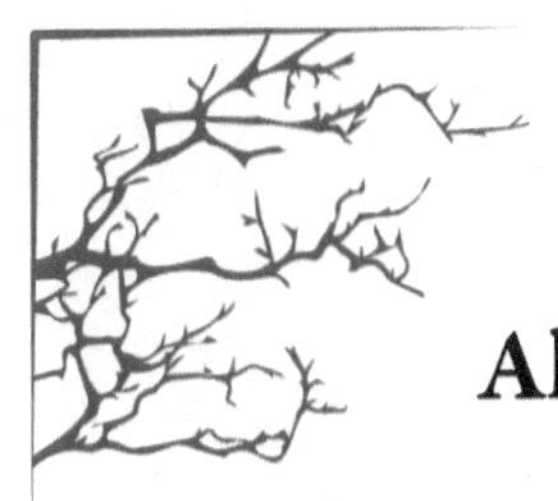

Also by Helen

Reactive Magic Series

Reactive

Magnetic

Volatile

Familiar Magic Series

Familiars and Foes

Accidents and Apparitions (published in Jingle Spells)

Curses and Cousins

Young Adult Books

Broken Silence

Underwater

We All Fall

Children's Books

The Trespassers Club

There's No Such Thing As Humans

Aunt Kelly's Dog

Jenny No-Knickers

Do Fruit Worry About Getting Fat?

Short Stories

Symbolic Death

Find out more at www.helenvfletcher.com

Coming soon...
Explosive: Reactive Magic Book 4
Will it end in flames?
Join Helen's mailing list at www.helenvfletcher.com to be one
of the first to read it.

About the Author

Helen Vivienne Fletcher is a children's and young adult author, spoken word poet and award-winning playwright. She has won and been shortlisted for numerous writing competitions including winning the Outstanding New Playwright Award at the Wellington Theatre Awards, making the shortlist for the Storylines Joy Cowley Award, and the finalist list for the Ngaio Marsh Best First Book Award.

Helen has worked in many jobs, doing everything from theatre stage management to phone counselling. She discovered her passion for writing for young people while working as a youth support worker, and now helps children find their own passion for storytelling through her work as a creative writing tutor.

She lives in Wellington with her disability assistance dog, Bindi – a five-year-old, playful Labrador who loves soft toys, cuddles, and can fit three tennis balls in her mouth at once.

Overall, Helen just loves telling stories and is always excited when people want to read or hear them.

Read more at https://www.helenvfletcher.com/.

9 781991 167248